"Are you pregna

Blaire gasped. Her face turned ashen. "What?"

"I asked—"

"I heard you." Blaire closed her eyes and turned around, then leaned back against her car.

"So it's true," Justin said, his voice going husky. "I'm the father, aren't I?"

She nodded. "Yes."

"So this is why you've been avoiding me. You weren't going to tell me at all, were you?"

"Justin, I'm sorry. I panicked. I didn't know what to do. I'm still not sure."

"Look, Blaire, this has taken us both by surprise, but we need to talk about it."

"There's nothing to talk about. We spent a wonderful night together, but you don't owe me anything. I don't plan to make demands of you. Don't trouble yourself about me one little bit. I'll be just fine. Now if you'll move your truck. I'd like to get back to work."

Justin stood there for a long moment, unable to move. He was going to be a father. Blaire Harding carried his child. And she wanted nothing to do with him....

Dear Reader,

Well, the lazy days of summer are winding to an end, so what better way to celebrate those last long beach afternoons than with a good book? We here at Silhouette Special Edition are always happy to oblige! We begin with *Diamonds and Deceptions* by Marie Ferrarella, the next in our continuity series, THE PARKS EMPIRE. When a mesmerizing man walks into her father's bookstore, sheltered Brooke Moss believes he's her dream come true. But he's about to challenge everything she thought she knew about her own family.

Victoria Pade continues her NORTHBRIDGE NUPTIALS with *Wedding Willies,* in which a runaway bride with an aversion to both small towns and matrimony finds herself falling for both, along with Northbridge's most eligible bachelor! In Patricia Kay's *Man of the Hour,* a woman finds her gratitude to the detective who found her missing child turning quickly to…love. In *Charlie's Angels* by Cheryl St. John, a single father is stymied when his little girl is convinced that finding a new mommy is as simple as having an angel sprinkle him with her "miracle dust"— until he meets the beautiful blonde who drives a rig called "Silver Angel." In *It Takes Three* by Teresa Southwick, a pregnant caterer sets her sights on the handsome single dad who swears his fatherhood days are behind him. Sure they are! And the MEN OF THE CHEROKEE ROSE series by Janis Reams Hudson concludes with *The Cowboy on Her Trail,* in which one night of passion with the man she's always wanted results in a baby on the way. Can marriage be far behind?

Enjoy all six of these wonderful novels, and please do come back next month for six more new selections, only from Silhouette Special Edition.

Gail Chasan
Senior Editor

Please address questions and book requests to:
Silhouette Reader Service
U.S.: 3010 Walden Ave., P.O. Box 1325, Buffalo, NY 14269
Canadian: P.O. Box 609, Fort Erie, Ont. L2A 5X3

The Cowboy on Her Trail

JANIS REAMS HUDSON

Silhouette®

SPECIAL EDITION™

Published by Silhouette Books

America's Publisher of Contemporary Romance

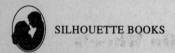

SILHOUETTE BOOKS

ISBN 0-373-24632-3

THE COWBOY ON HER TRAIL

Copyright © 2004 by Janis Reams Hudson

This edition published by arrangement with Harlequin Books S.A.

® and TM are trademarks of Harlequin Books S.A., used under license.
Trademarks indicated with ® are registered in the United States Patent
and Trademark Office, the Canadian Trade Marks Office and in other
countries.

Visit Silhouette Books at www.eHarlequin.com

Printed in U.S.A.

Books by Janis Reams Hudson

Silhouette Special Edition

Resist Me if You Can #1037
The Mother of His Son #1095
His Daughter's Laughter #1105
Until You #1210
Their Other Mother #1267
The Price of Honor #1332
A Child on the Way #1349
Daughter on His Doorstep #1434
The Last Wilder #1474
†*The Daddy Survey* #1619
†*The Other Brother* #1626
†*The Cowboy on Her Trail* #1632

*Wilders of Wyatt County
†Men of the Cherokee Rose

JANIS REAMS HUDSON

was born in California, grew up in Colorado, lived in Texas for a few years and now calls central Oklahoma home. She is the author of more than twenty-five novels, both contemporary and historical romances. Her books have appeared on the Waldenbooks, B. Dalton and BookRak bestseller lists and earned numerous awards, including the National Reader's Choice Award and Reviewer's Choice awards from *Romantic Times*. She is a three-time finalist for the coveted RITA® Award from Romance Writers of America and is a past president of RWA.

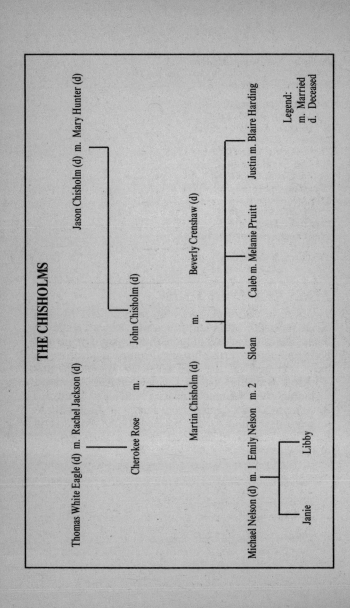

THE CHISHOLMS

Thomas White Eagle (d) m. Rachel Jackson (d)

Jason Chisholm (d) m. Mary Hunter (d)

Cherokee Rose m. John Chisholm (d)

Martin Chisholm (d)

Beverly Crenshaw (d) m.

Sloan   Caleb m. Melanie Pruitt   Justin m. Blaire Harding

Michael Nelson (d) m. 1 Emily Nelson m. 2

Janie   Libby

Legend:
m. Married
d. Deceased

Prologue

Somewhere, sometime in his life, Justin Chisholm figured he must have done something incredibly right, and this night was his reward. He couldn't fathom any other reason why he should be so lucky as to finally end up with Blaire Harding in his bed.

He knew she was in his bed because they had just made sweet, hot love together, and he was just now drifting down from a peak higher than he'd ever known.

The fact that it was the motel's bed rather than his own didn't faze him a bit. He was paying for the bed, so that made it his, right?

When a man lived in his family home with his grandmother, his brother, sister-in-law and two young nieces, not to mention the housekeeper, her husband, and their baby, he didn't take a woman home to his own personal bed. Not if he expected any privacy. Not if he had any respect for his family and the woman, and this was a woman for whom he had plenty of respect.

He didn't need to open his eyes to see the shape of her, sleek and curved in all the right places, lean where she should be, round where it counted. Behind his closed lids he could still see her dark blond hair, her golden brown eyes. The cute way the tip of her nose turned slightly upward, which she thought made her look like a Pekingese and he thought made her look adorably kissable.

He couldn't remember a time in the past several months since she'd moved back to town when he hadn't wanted her. She'd made him wait, she'd put him off, she'd kept him at arm's length all that time.

But gradually she had let him get closer. A conversation or two. A developing friendship. Eventually, a ride to get her car fixed. A lunch with a bunch of their mutual friends. A dance or two at the local watering hole. Then another dance, and another, until finally she had agreed to go out to dinner with him. Then dinner and a movie.

No woman before her had ever made him work so hard to please her. But he wanted to please her, in every way he could.

Tonight she'd finally agreed to let them please each other.

With a low moan, he inhaled the fragrance of wildflowers in her hair. "You smell so good."

Curled up warmly against his chest, Blaire Harding smiled and sighed. "Glad you approve."

"Oh, I do." He nuzzled his face against her hair. Then, when she expected something deeply romantic, or maybe a sweet word or two, or even a comfortable silence, he snorted in her ear.

Blaire burst out laughing and rolled away from him with a shriek. "Where'd he go? Where'd he go?"

"Where'd who go?" He sat up in bed and looked quickly around the room.

"Justin Chisholm," she cried. "He was here just a minute ago, then all of a sudden there was a pig snorting in my ear."

"Oh, ha-ha." He pulled her back against his chest. "I don't know how to coo like a turtledove, or whatever."

"So you snorted?"

He reached over and turned on the bedside lamp. "Maybe that was an allergic reaction."

"To what, me?"

"To wildflowers."

Blaire squinted and tried to duck away from the glare. "Egad, that's bright. What wildflowers?"

"The ones I smell in your hair."

"You said it smelled good."

"It does."

"But it makes you snort?"

"Maybe."

She laughed and wrapped her arms around his neck. "I think you were just trying to be funny. And it worked, I guess, because it made me laugh."

They lay nestled together, still feeling the afterglow of two thorough rounds of intense lovemaking. After several minutes Justin shifted and groaned.

"Uh, Blaire," he said, "believe me, this is the absolute last thing on earth I want to say to you right now…"

Blaire's stomach tightened. After months of denying herself the pleasure of accepting any of his numerous invitations, she had finally given in and spent the most incredible night of her life with a man she'd had a secret crush on forever, and he was going to tell her he didn't want to see her again. She just knew it.

But Blaire knew how to be practical. Better to get the bad news over with and get on with her life. She pulled her arms from around his neck. She moved to push away from him, but he held her close.

"But you're going to say it anyway," she said tensely.

"Only because of an overdeveloped sense of honesty, which I often wish my grandmother had never drummed into me."

She couldn't look him in the face. Not if he was going to tell her he didn't want to see her again. "Honesty's never a bad thing. Why don't you just spit it out and get it over with?"

"Okay." He lowered his forehead to rest against hers. "You said you wanted to be home by two. It's one-thirty."

A wave of relief swept through her and left her limp in his arms. "Oh," she managed.

Justin sensed that something wasn't quite right. He frowned. "What did you think I was going to say?"

She turned her face away and shook her head. "Nothing."

"Blaire? What's wrong?"

"Wrong?" She managed a smile and rolled over to sit on the side of the bed with her back to him. "What could be wrong?" Holding a corner of the sheet over her breasts, which was a ridiculous attempt at belated modesty considering what they'd been doing to and with each other for the past couple of hours, she smiled at him over her shoulder. "It feels silly to say I had a great time, but I did."

He sat up behind her and kissed her bare shoulder.

A shiver of remembered passion raced through her.

"It doesn't sound silly to me," he said.

Blaire noted the time on the clock on the cheap dresser across the room, 1:35 a.m.

When they'd made their date the other day she'd told him she wanted to be home by 2:00 a.m. and made him promise he would not try to get her to change her mind. She was pleased that he was sticking to that.

She had no pressing reason for getting home by

two, except she wouldn't have the luxury of sleeping late in the morning. Her father always opened the feed store at seven every morning, Monday through Saturday, and tomorrow was Saturday. Her job was to man the office, so she had to be there during business hours.

Without thought she glanced down at her wristwatch—the only thing she was wearing.

How odd, she thought with irritation. Her watch had stopped at 11:30 p.m. It had lasted through their first round of lovemaking, but not the second.

The implications suddenly struck her. She bolted upright. It couldn't be. This had to be a coincidence.

"What's wrong?" Justin asked, his lips moving over the back of her neck. "You're all of a sudden stiff as a board." He ran his hands up and down her arms. "I told you I'd get you home on time."

"It's not that. It's nothing." Her mind scrambled for something to say that would make sense and justify her sudden stiffness, which she could not deny. "Just a cramp in my foot."

"Ouch. I hate it when that happens. Here." He slid from behind her and knelt—naked—at her feet. "Which foot?"

He sure was pretty to look at, in all his naked glory. Flat stomach, hard, lean muscles, light bronze skin speaking of his Cherokee ancestry, with his face, neck and hands several shades darker from working outdoors all year on his ranch. Then there were those parts of him that declared he was a man. All man.

"Blaire?"

"Hmm? Oh. This one." She lifted her right foot, ashamed of herself for lying, but what was a girl to do?

She glanced at her watch again. It hadn't advanced a second. She noticed Justin's watch lying on the nightstand. Desperate to prove to herself that her watch stopping at this particular time was merely a coincidence, she grabbed his and strapped it onto her wrist just above her watch. It was an old-fashioned watch with a face and a second hand, the kind of watch you had to wind. On the tightest notch of the brown leather strap it fit her like a large, loose bracelet.

"That's a little big for you."

"Mmm."

She didn't have a cramp in her foot, but his hands still felt like magic as they worked her instep. "Mmm."

The smile he gave her, kneeling there at her feet without a stitch of clothing on, was pure devil. "Like that, do you?"

She smiled back. "What do you think?"

"I think if you keep looking at me like that, you're gonna get mad at me for making you miss that two o'clock deadline you set for yourself."

Blaire let out a sigh. "You just ruined the mood."

He shook his head ruefully. "Damn my hide."

The clock on the dresser said it was 1:45 a.m.

Her watch still said 11:30 p.m.

His watch, which a few minutes ago had read the same as the clock on the dresser, now read 1:42 a.m. The second hand was not moving. It had stopped, apparently, the moment she put it on.

Blaire swallowed. Hard. A fine trembling started in her shoulders and raced down her arms to leave her hands unsteady. She unbuckled the leather band and placed his watch back on the bedside table. She stared at it, and as if by her will alone, the second hand resumed ticking its way around the face.

Cold sweat broke out along Blaine's spine.

Don't panic. Stay calm. It doesn't mean anything. It's just a family myth. A silly coincidence. There's no way—

"Blaire?"

She jumped as if shot. "What?"

"Babe, what's wrong? You look like you've seen a ghost."

"What? Oh. Sorry. I...I must be coming down with something." She pulled her foot from his grasp and bunched the sheet around herself as she scooted off the bed and started grabbing her clothes from the floor. "I've got to get home."

What good she thought getting herself home was going to do was beyond her. If the family myth about watches not working turned out to be true, she was screwed. In more ways than one.

Justin watched her as she scrambled into her

clothes as if her life depended on it. By the time she'd finished dressing, so had he. He grabbed his watch from the bedside table and strapped it on, frowning to note that it seemed to be slow when compared to the two dollar, digital alarm clock bolted to the dresser. He could have sworn they'd been in sync a couple of hours ago.

As he followed Blaire to the door he glanced around the cheap motel room and cringed. Maybe what Blaire was suffering from was a bad case of second thoughts. The room was clean, with fairly new although cheap furnishings, but there was no disguising it from the motel room it was.

She deserved better than this dinky room. They both did. But she hadn't invited him to her place, and he didn't have a "place." Hell, he didn't even have a back seat; he drove a pickup.

With her overcoat on to shield her from the chilly December wind, she reached for the doorknob, but he put his hand over hers and paused. "You going to be able to make it home? Do you need a doctor or something?"

"No, no, it's nothing like that." She gave him a small smile. "I'll be fine once I get home. Please." She removed her hand from the doorknob and placed it on his arm. "Please don't worry. I had a wonderful night, and now it's time for me to go home. That's all."

He studied her closely. Her color seemed more normal now than it had a few minutes ago. "You're sure?"

"I'm sure."

"Come on, then." He opened the door and slipped his arm around her shoulders. "Let's get you home."

Chapter One

It was a chilly February night on the Cherokee Rose ranch in Central Oklahoma. Cherokee Rose Chisholm took a well-earned rest in her recliner before the big screen TV in the living room.

She could take the time to relax because she'd been in the saddle most of the day, and at the desk working on the ranch records and books half the evening.

Thank God, she thought, for Maria, who'd stepped into the position of housekeeper when Earline retired last month, and for Emily, who loved to oversee the house and meals and added a much-needed feminine touch to the house. Between those two women, they took a load of responsibility off

Rose's shoulders. And their daughters—six-year-old Libby and eight-year-old Janie, Rose's new grand-daughters, plus Rosa, Maria's new baby, who was named for the ranch on which she was born. Rose had feared having a newborn in the house would wear them all out. At seventy-eight, Rose was quite certain that she was not up to sharing her home with a newborn.

But Maria was so good with the baby, and Emily helped her a great deal, that all Rose had to do was hold the baby and coo over her when she was sleepy and sweet-smelling.

With her two oldest grandsons married now, that left only Justin, and Rose was getting concerned about him. She'd thought he'd found someone spe-cial a couple of months ago, but lately he'd been moping around a lot, and moping was simply not in Justin's nature.

If he didn't snap out of it soon, she would just have to stick her nose in. She couldn't bear to see one of her boys unhappy.

"Hi, this is Blaire. I can't come to the phone right now. If you want me to call you back, leave a message."

Justin resisted the urge to pound his head against the wall. He hung up without leaving a message. If he left any more messages he'd end up getting ar-rested as a stalker.

Two months. Two damn months he'd been trying

to get close to Blaire again. Two damn months of excuses, of lost messages, of unreturned phone calls.

He had called her the day after they spent the night together to make sure she was all right, since she'd thought she might be coming down with something. She'd said she was fine, nothing a good night's sleep hadn't been able to take care of. She'd sounded fine, as far as that went. Until he'd asked to see her again.

The excuses had started with that first morning-after phone call. Her cousin in Ponca City was sick and Blaire was going up there for the weekend to help her out.

She couldn't go out the next week because she and her mother were spending the weekend in Oklahoma City doing last-minute Christmas shopping.

She couldn't go out the next week because she was going to spend the whole week with her grandmother down in Ardmore so the woman wouldn't be alone over the holidays.

After that, her father had a bad case of the flu, so she had to help take up the slack at the feed store, and help her mother take care of her father.

When her father got well, her mother came down with it.

When her mother got well, Blaire came down with it.

Justin had to admit that as excuses went, she had some good ones. But they'd spent the night together in early December. It was now the first week of February. He was starting to get the message. It was finally coming in loud and clear. The woman wanted nothing more to do with him.

He wondered what it said about him that it took him two months for it to finally sink in, but he wasn't used to rejection. It hadn't happened often enough for him to easily recognize it.

And dammit, it stung, being rejected. He couldn't say he cared for it.

"Whasa matter, Uncle Justin?" Six-year-old Libby, his brother Sloan's new stepdaughter, leaned against the jamb of his open door. "You look all sad."

"Who, me?" He clipped his cell phone back to his belt and stood up. "Naw, not me."

Libby bounced into the room and straightened the bedspread he'd just been sitting on.

"Thanks, sweets."

"You're welcome."

"What are you doing up here? I thought you guys were watching TV."

"We are." When she smiled, her whole face beamed. "Daddy's making popcorn. Mama said to let you know so you could have some, too, if you wanted."

"If I wanted? Of course I want. Let's go."

It still gave him a hell of a kick to hear Libby or Janie call his oldest brother Daddy. It probably tickled him almost as much as it tickled Sloan to have the new title.

Everybody around him was getting married, he thought as he followed Libby downstairs to the living room. First Sloan and Emily last summer, then his middle brother Caleb and Melanie, their nearest neighbor and lifelong friend.

Caleb and Melanie lived at her family ranch, Pruitt Ranch, over on the next section. Caleb had been there since their wedding back in December. It was the first time that all three Chisholm brothers had not lived under the same roof since the day they were born. It seemed odd.

But that in no way meant the house was quieter due to Caleb's absence, Justin thought with a silent chuckle as he rounded the corner into the mayhem of the kitchen. Emily and her two daughters—all three with blond hair and blue eyes, amid a houseful of black-haired, dark-eyed Indians—more than made up for Caleb's absence.

Especially since Emily liked to cook, and Caleb hadn't.

And Emily would box his ears if he ever said such a thing out loud. That is, if Grandmother didn't get to him first.

"There you two are." Emily wiped her hands on the dish towel wrapped around her waist. "We were wondering what was keeping you. Is that popcorn almost ready?" she added to Sloan, who manned the microwave.

"Just relax," Sloan said over the popping of the

corn inside the microwave. "Some things can't be rushed."

"Oh, aren't you funny." Behind his back, Emily made a comical face at him.

Janie and Libby burst into giggles.

Emily darted them a look and placed a finger over her lips, asking for their silence.

"Counting down," Sloan said.

The two little girls snuggled up on each side of him and counted down with the numbers on the microwave panel.

"Six, five, four, three, two, one. Ding!"

"Okay, that's one. Here's bag number two." Emily tossed a second package of unpopped corn to Sloan.

Snack time—assembly style—on the Cherokee Rose.

Watching Sloan with his new family brought an ache to Justin's belly that stunned him, dismayed him. Was there a part of him that wanted to get married and start a family of his own?

The idea wasn't out of the realm of possibility, and it wasn't as if the word *marriage* hadn't popped into his head a number of times in the past several months, but always in regard to his brothers, never to himself. He was only twenty-eight, for cripes sake. He didn't need to get in any hurry about it.

But whenever he saw what his brothers had, he got this funny emptiness, as if some part of him wasn't yet finished.

A couple of months ago he'd thought maybe that had something to do with Blaire Harding.

Since she now wanted nothing to do with him, he figured if she did have anything to do with that empty spot inside him, it was going to stay empty for a long damn time.

"What's with you these days, kid?"

Justin glanced around the room and realized he and Sloan were alone in the kitchen. He must have spaced out for quite a while, lost in his own thoughts, not to have noticed that Emily and the kids had gone back to the living room. Sloan leaned against the counter, his arms folded across his chest, one stockinged foot crossed over the other one. His gaze was like a laser, zeroing in on Justin with deep intensity.

"You've been moping around the place for days, maybe weeks, and that's not like you. Wanna talk about it?"

Justin stuffed his fingers into his hip pockets. "Nope."

One of Sloan's eyebrows hitched up his forehead. "Nope?"

"That's right. Nope."

"Fine by me." Sloan shrugged. "Just be aware that if you don't talk to me about whatever it is that's bugging you, Grandmother or Emily or both of them are going to be after you. They're worried about you."

Justin frowned. "What are they worried about?

I'm here, I'm eating and sleeping just fine, I'm doing my work, pulling my weight. What's the big deal?"

"The big deal," Sloan said, pulling away from the counter to stand on both feet, "is that while you're doing all of those normal, everyday things, you're moping."

"Moping?"

"And you're starting to sound like a parrot."

"Parrot?"

Sloan's lips twitched. "Come on, give me something to tell them, or I'll make something up."

"Oh, yeah?" This should be good. "Go ahead, big guy, make something up."

"Okay, I'll tell them you're pining away for a woman."

Justin ran his tongue over his teeth. "A woman."

"Sure. Why else would a fun-loving guy like you start looking all hangdog, like you just lost your best friend?"

"Is that the best you can do?"

"I suppose I could tell them you've got hemorrhoids."

Justin whooped with laughter. God, he loved this brother of his.

"What's all the noise in there?" their grandmother called. "You two are missing the movie."

Justin slung an arm over his big brother's shoulder. "We're coming, Grandmother, oh love of my life."

Rose Chisholm made a snorting noise. "If I'm the

love of your life, no wonder you've been moping around the place for weeks."

"Oh, but Grandmother!" Justin leaned over her recliner, bracing himself on the arms of the chair, and planted a wet, sloppy kiss on her cheek. "You are my sunshine. The light of my life. My reason for being. You're the jam in my jelly roll."

Libby and Janie giggled, while Rose tried to shoo him away like he was a pesky fly.

"Get on with you," she said, her lips twitching.

"But Grandmother, I love you. Let me count the ways."

"I'll count your ways, young man. Sit down and hush up. Cruella's about to get her hands on the puppies."

Justin had casually claimed to Sloan that he was sleeping fine. At one o'clock that morning he kicked back the covers, realizing that, for this night at least, he'd lied.

Grandmother swore by warm milk. He didn't think he could choke down warm milk, but a glass of cold might help. He stepped into his jeans and pulled on a flannel shirt against the nighttime chill of the house, and against the off chance of running into a female.

The place was crawling with females these days. His grandmother had always been there, of course. She had raised him and his brothers since their parents died when Justin was a baby. But no other female had lived under their roof until Sloan brought Emily home with him.

Then there was Emily, and her two little girls.

A couple of months ago, they'd added Maria and baby Rosa to the mix. They and Maria's husband, Pedro, were living in the spare room downstairs, where Justin had moved when he gave his room upstairs over to the girls. Then Caleb had left, so Justin moved back upstairs and Maria, Pedro and Rosa moved in.

Musical bedrooms. But lots of females, and Justin liked it that way, even if it did mean he had to make sure he was dressed before he dared step out of his room or even open his door. A small price to pay, he knew, for the company of so many lovely women.

Who needed one specific, special woman, he told himself as he crept down the stairs in the dark, when he was surrounded at home by so many very special ladies?

One of whom he scared the fire out of when he rounded the corner into the kitchen and spoke.

"Emily?"

"Oh! God! Justin. You took ten years off my life."

"I'm sorry. What are you doing sneaking around down here in the dark in the middle of the night?"

"Shh," she said putting a finger to her lips. She turned on the small light over the stove. "You'll wake Rosa and her parents." Their room was down a short hall off the back of the kitchen. "And I could ask you the same question."

"I couldn't sleep. Thought I'd give a glass of milk a try. But I would have turned on the light once I got here. You didn't. That's why I didn't know you were here, which is why I was so quiet, so I wouldn't wake anybody up, when you were already awake and sneaking around—"

"Justin."

"Huh?"

"I've never heard you ramble before."

Justin took a deep breath and let it out. "I'm not sure I've ever done it before. I don't know why I did this time."

"Maybe so I wouldn't ask you the inevitable question," she said gently. She turned away and took the milk out of the fridge and poured them each a glass.

"Thanks." He took a glass from her, then pulled a chair away from the table for her.

She took her seat, then he took his.

"You're not going to ask me what question I'm talking about?" she asked.

Justin sipped his milk, then used his forefinger to wipe his upper lip. "A lot of questions are inevitable. I'm sure you'll come up with one."

"I'm sorry. I'm prying."

"Oh, no." He reached across the table and took her hand. "No, I didn't mean it like that. Emily, I love it that you care enough about me to worry. I just don't like to see you worry, because there's nothing to worry about."

She gave his hand a return squeeze. "Justin, how long have I lived in this house with you and your family?"

He shrugged. "I don't know. Seven or eight months."

"That's right. Now, don't you think during that time I've come to know you pretty well?"

"Okay, I can see where this is going. Yes, you know me pretty well."

"Which means I can tell when you're not quite yourself. And Justin? You haven't been yourself for several weeks. I just want you to know that one of the perks of having a sister-in-law, especially one who lives in the same house with you, is that you can dump your troubles on her, and she'll listen. She might even be able to give you the female take on things."

"The female take on things?"

"Yes. You know what I mean. Let's say a man and a woman are driving down the road and up ahead they see a nice restaurant. The woman says, 'Oh, look. Do you want to stop there for dinner?' The man thinks about it a minute, then says, 'No.' The woman gets her feelings hurt and sulks all night, then the man gets mad at her sulking, and before the night's over, they have a whopping big fight, and neither of them has a clue what went wrong."

Justin took another swallow of milk, thinking he was going to enjoy this late night interlude. Emily was so earnest in her effort to help him. He couldn't wait to see what she came up with.

"Okay," he said. "I'll bite. What went wrong? Seems to me she was too sensitive, getting her feelings hurt over a restaurant."

"Well, yes and no. You see, when a woman asks if you want to eat somewhere in particular, or go to a specific place, or see a certain movie, she's not simply asking your opinion. What she's really saying is, 'I'd like to eat at that restaurant. How about it?' Or 'I'd like to see this movie. Will you take me?'"

"I guess that makes sense."

"Yes, but that's not what a man hears. A man hears the words she uses, and not the underlying meaning. He hears a question that asks his opinion, and he gives his opinion."

"So why doesn't the woman say she wants to eat at that place instead of asking him if he wants to?"

"Because even in the twenty-first century, little girls are still taught not to put themselves and their wants forward. That they're supposed to cater to everyone else's wishes before their own. If someone else wants to see a movie you don't care for, you go see it anyway. Particularly if it's your date. If you don't like the movie he picks, he might think that means you don't like him."

"Well, that's just plain stupid."

"You're telling me."

"Why do parents teach little girls to be submissive like that?"

"Because that's how they were raised, I guess.

But they've done studies, too, on young children going to school for the first time, and inevitably the girls are quiet and calm and the boys are loud and aggressive, demanding the teacher's attention. Maybe some of it's genetic—God forbid and cut out my tongue for even saying it."

Justin chuckled. "Your secret's safe with me."

"Anyway." She waved away the idea. "My point was—"

He grinned at her. "You had a point?"

She gave him a mock scowl. "My point in all this is that sometimes great big problems, or what seem like great big problems, can stem from the smallest misunderstanding simply because men and women use language differently."

"I'm sure you're right."

"Take that one step further, and keep in mind that I'm a woman."

"Oh, honey, I know you are."

She rolled her eyes toward the ceiling. "I mean, I can give you the female perspective on a situation, should you happen to need it."

"I appreciate it. I really do."

"And if none of this is to the point," she said, her lips twitching. "If you really don't have woman trouble, there's a tube of Preparation H in the bathroom medicine chest upstairs."

Justin lowered his head to the table and groaned. "Do you think Grandmother would notice if Sloan just disappeared? I could tie bricks around his neck and stuff him in the pond. That'd work."

Emily laughed softly in the dim light. "Stubborn, stubborn man. You're not going to tell me what's bothering you, are you?"

"Thank you," he said, "for asking. For caring. You're right, it's a woman, but she doesn't want anything to do with me, so that's the end of that."

"Who is it?"

Justin shook his head. "My lips are sealed."

"Good for you. You get extra points for that."

"I do?"

"You do. What makes you think she doesn't want anything to do with you?"

Justin gave her a wry smile. "She won't take my calls, won't return my calls. When she sees me coming she heads the other way."

Emily frowned. "What does she say when you ask her about all this?"

"Say?" he cried. "She doesn't say anything, because I can't get near her."

"And you *like* this woman?"

Justin chuckled and shook his head. "Oh, yeah. I really like her. And that's the thing, Emily. When we were together, I know she felt the same way. We were damn near perfect together."

"Wow."

"Yeah, wow is right," he said. "Then, poof. It's all over, no word, no explanation, no nothing."

"Wait a minute. She broke it off with you without saying *anything?*"

"Without one stinking word," he said with disgust.

Emily reached across the table and placed her hand over the back of his. "Justin, if she hasn't got the guts to tell you face-to-face that she doesn't want to see you anymore, then she's not good enough for you."

"Ah, come on—"

"No, you come on. Think about it. Do you really want to tie yourself, even temporarily, to a woman who may or may not have a legitimate complaint against you, but who'll never tell you?"

To this woman, Justin thought, yes. Yes, he did. He thought.

"She's either too shy, too scared, or too self-centered to consider your side of things. Or, and believe me, I hate to say this, she simply doesn't care what you think or how you feel."

"No." He shook his head. "I can't believe that. Not of her. She's not like that."

"She's not? Or you don't want her to be?" Emily asked gently.

"Boy, you're tough, lady."

"No, I'm just not emotionally involved with her the way you are. I'm on your side, looking out for your best interests. You're on her side. There's a big difference."

"Yeah, I know. But you don't need to worry about me anymore. I've decided to give up and move on."

"Have you?"

"I have. Honest Injun." He held one hand up, palm out.

"Oh, bad." She groaned and rolled her eyes at the tacky phrase he and his brothers—his Native American brothers, she sometimes reminded them, much to their amusement—tossed at each other whenever it suited them. "Bad, bad Justin."

However, Emily admitted, when one of the Chisholm brothers said *Honest Injun,* it was as good as taking an oath with one hand on the Bible. They meant it.

Unless, of course, there was a certain look in their eyes, or a quirk to their lips, or their fingers were crossed behind their back. But then it was always meant in teasing fun rather than an out-and-out lie. Like saying, "Oh, yeah, suuure." *Wink wink.*

She couldn't see any of the telltale signs of joking on Justin now, and both his hands were in plain sight, fingers uncrossed. He must be serious. He really had decided to give up on this mystery woman and move on.

"Are you okay with that?" she asked.

"I guess I have to be, don't I?"

And when Justin said it, he meant it. He was through beating his head against the brick wall of Blaire's unexplained indifference.

Who needed her, anyway? She damn sure wasn't the only fish in the sea, peanut in the can, cookie in the jar, straw in the damn bale. Woman in the world.

But damn her beautiful hide, he wanted to know why. And he wanted her to look him in the eye and tell him. And by Jove, she would do it.

Chapter Two

Blaire Harding surreptitiously wiped her damp palms against her wool skirt and followed her parents down the aisle and into their regular pew at the Rose Rock Baptist Church because she'd been unable to come up with a good enough excuse to stay home.

Not that she didn't want to go to church. She enjoyed church. It uplifted her, helped her end one week and gird her loins, as it were, for the next.

But why did it have to be this church? The one where, every single solitary week, the entire Chisholm clan, which was growing by the month, filled the second center pew from one end to the other.

She was running out of excuses there, too. With Justin. Every time she thought of him she was swamped by a dozen different emotions. Pleasure. Arousal. Anticipation. Guilt. Hopelessness. Terror. Resignation. Yearning. And more guilt.

What was she to do about him?

Her mother entered the pew first, then her father. Blaire followed and sat next to him, her gaze drawn against her will to those broad, suede-clad shoulders belonging to Justin Chisholm five pews up. She knew exactly how wide those shoulders were. She'd felt them, every inch, front and back and all around, her hands against his hot bare flesh.

Any more thoughts like that, she thought, her cheeks stinging, and a lightning bolt was going to strike right through the beamed ceiling of the church.

In the second row from the front, Justin felt her gaze on his back as if she were stroking him. He stood it through the opening hymn, through the announcements, the opening prayer. But as the pastor began his sermon on sins of the flesh—why did the sermons always seem aimed at him personally?—Justin couldn't take it any longer. He turned and glanced back over his shoulder.

She was there. He'd known she was. Her hair was pulled back and tied at her nape with a clip of some sort. The style gave her a soft, fragile appearance. Especially with that telltale blush staining her cheeks, the stark look in those golden brown eyes before she glanced away.

Guilt? Was that what he'd seen in her eyes?

By damn—*sorry, Lord*—he'd had enough of this. He was going to get answers out of her or die trying.

When church let out—at 12:25 p.m. because Reverend Conners didn't know the meaning of "on time," Lord love him—Justin made for the door as fast as he could without bowling anyone down, but he was still too late.

Blaire and her parents were gone.

Justin bit back a curse. This was Sunday; he should be able to do better with his language at least on Sunday. But dammit, he wanted to talk to her. He had to know what that look meant, because it had looked to him like the look a woman gives a man she wants to be close to.

"Justin," his grandmother called. "Are you coming to dinner?"

"I'm coming." Every Sunday after church the Chisholm family went to Lucille's on Main for dinner. The Chisholms, and everyone else in town, it seemed. Caleb and Melanie were with them today. It was the only time during the week that they were all together as a family.

Family meant a lot to Justin. Maybe because he'd grown up without parents. His brothers and grandmother had been his family. They were everything to him. It seemed odd to him that Caleb no longer lived at home, but they were grown men now, not boys. It was time for them to see what they could make of themselves.

But Justin had always thought that the "making of themselves" would be done right there on the Cherokee Rose. That was home to him, to all of them. His soul was rooted in the land that first Chisholm staked out after surviving the horrors of the Trail of Tears.

The ranch had changed in size from time to time, depending on the direction of the winds of fortune and the ability of any given generation to hold on through lean times and flourish in good times.

The Rose was Justin's home.

When Caleb had moved to the PR with Melanie, it had been a jolt for Justin. He'd never really thought about any of them leaving the ranch.

Then, too, Melanie had been Justin's running mate, his buddy, his playmate, for most of his life. She was still and always would be his friend, but he doubted if she'd want to help him TP the mayor's house when that new city sales tax went into effect next month. In the old days, she'd have been the ringleader of such a gag. Now she was his brother's wife.

But at least the PR was right next door, so to speak, so that wasn't too bad. He could see Caleb and Mel whenever he wanted. Hell, they had even installed a gate in a stretch of fence common to both ranches, so they could get from one house to the other on horseback as the crow flies.

Yes, the Rose was Justin's home.

So why was he starting to feel like the odd man out?

Lucille's was packed, as was usual on a Sunday afternoon. But among the dozens of diners there was no Harding family.

Justin ground his back teeth together in frustration. Blaire and her parents used to come here every Sunday after church. He couldn't remember the number of times he'd seen them there. Now, however, when he wanted to talk to her, they weren't there.

"You look like you could chew nails."

Justin jerked and knocked his elbow against Melanie's arm. "Oh. Sorry. What?" Melanie Pruitt Chisholm was Justin's newest sister-in-law. She and her parents had been their closest neighbors forever. Mel and Justin had been best pals their entire lives. Now they were family, and that was fitting. He had loved her like a sister for years. There was nothing they couldn't say to each other, nothing they wouldn't do for each other.

She nudged him back with her elbow. "You could scare little kids with that look, pal. You practice it in the mirror?"

"Did you rehearse that joke? Maybe try it out on the cows first before you take it out on the road?"

"Quick," Sloan said from across the table. "Somebody separate those two before they start a food fight."

Justin and Melanie gave him twin mock looks of innocence. Each put a hand to the chest and cried, *"Moi?"*

The conversation halted then because the waitress arrived with their orders. After the food was distributed and everyone dug in, Melanie gave Justin a smirk.

"So," she said between bites of Lucille's infamous spaghetti. "I hear you've got hemorrhoids."

Justin nearly spewed a mouthful of tea across the table.

"Oh, I am going to enjoy getting even for that." He included Melanie, Sloan and Emily in his warning. "You won't know where, you won't know when. You won't even know how. But one day, suddenly you'll realize that I got you back. All of you."

"Oooh," Sloan said in a high falsetto. "I'm shaking in my boots."

"Yeah," Melanie said with a sneer. "I'm gonna lose a lot of sleep over it myself."

Emily merely shook her head and smiled.

By the next day Justin was more determined than ever to confront Blaire. That look he'd caught on her face in church had stayed with him all day Sunday, and he'd lain awake half the night trying to figure out what it meant, why she would look at him that way, yet refuse to speak to him.

He was tired of guessing. It was time she gave him

some answers. Maybe then he could get her out of his system once and for all.

He pulled up around 9:00 a.m. at the feed store and went directly toward the office in back where Blaire took care of the store's bookkeeping. Just outside her half-open door Justin was stopped cold by the furious voices coming from within.

"Don't you go blaming this on me, by damn." That was Thomas Harding, Blaire's father, speaking. "Like mother, like daughter."

"What are you saying?" This frigid response came from Nancy, Blaire's mother.

"You know exactly what I'm saying. You got knocked up, now so has she. Like mother, like daughter. Her watch won't even run on her arm anymore."

Justin reached for the wall to steady himself. Knocked up? Blaire was pregnant? Watch? What watch?

"I *got* knocked up?" her mother shrieked. "Why you clueless, thickheaded piece of frog bait, who the hell was it who knocked me up? It takes two to tango, mister."

"You shoulda been on the damn pill and you know it."

"Oh, that's right, it's all my fault. You were just an innocent bystander."

"I never said any such thing. I married you, didn't I?"

"Yeah, and you haven't let me forget it for one single day since."

"I'll tell you one thing, Nancy girl. If I ever find out who did this to our little girl I'm gonna tear him to pieces with my bare hands. Right after I've made sure they're good and married. She'll make a pretty widow."

Justin gulped. Holly Hannah. Tom sounded like he meant every bloodthirsty word.

Discretion being the better part of valor, he decided it was time for a hasty—and silent—retreat.

Back out in his pickup, Justin sat a minute to catch his breath and let his head stop spinning.

Blaire was pregnant? *Pregnant?*

From what he'd seen of her in the past year or so—and he'd seen plenty, because he'd had his eye on her for at least that long—the only man who'd been near her in ages was…himself.

If she was pregnant, as far as he could tell, he was the father. They'd used a condom, but those weren't foolproof.

Father?

He shook his head hard. His heart was pounding at three times its normal speed. It took him two tries to get his key in the ignition, his hand shook so badly.

There was no question now. He had to talk to her. And he would, if it meant tearing this whole damn town apart to find her.

She hadn't been at the feed store. She could have

been at her parents' house behind the store for some reason, or at her apartment above their detached garage. But he didn't see her faded red compact in its usual spot next to the garage, so he figured she'd gone out to run an errand.

It was early, but maybe she was meeting a girlfriend for coffee. He drove through the parking lot of Lucille's, but her car wasn't there. Neither was it at either of the other two cafés, or at the burger place.

He tried the grocery store, but didn't see her there, either.

He was about to give up and go back and demand her parents tell him where she was when he spotted her coming out of the hardware store.

Considering how slippery she'd been for the past couple of months, he pulled up behind her faded red compact car and blocked her in so she couldn't leave. He killed his engine and pocketed the keys before getting out.

The sky was crystal blue, the air almost balmy for early February, the temperature hovering in the mid forties. But the slight breeze out of the north had a little nip to it, warning of another cold snap on the way.

Blaire stopped next to her car and stared at him, a small paper sack clutched in one fist. Her chest rose and fell rapidly. Her tongue flicked out and moistened her lips. It was a gesture of nerves, that much was obvious. But it still made Justin want to follow her tongue with his own.

"Justin."

"Blaire." He rounded her car and stopped five feet away from her. She was just as beautiful as he remembered. Her dark blond hair turned honey gold in the sun, a shade that matched her eyes, narrowed now, and wary as they studied him, then darted away. She looked as if she might want to turn and run, but to her credit, she stood her ground.

"What do you want?" she asked.

Justin gave a harsh laugh. "Maybe if you'd returned any one of my dozens of calls during the past weeks you might know."

"You're upset because I haven't called you back? Is that what this is about?"

"What do you mean, *this?* Can't a man stop and say hi to a woman he once spent a remarkable night with?"

The blush that stained her cheeks did his heart good.

The way she glanced sharply around to see if anyone might have overheard knocked a hole in what was left of his ego.

"What do you want, Justin? I've got to get back to the store."

He supposed if he wanted a straight answer about anything, he was going to have to ask a straight question. He stuck his hands into his coat pockets and clenched his fists. "Are you pregnant?"

Blaire gasped and took a step back. Her face turned ashen. "What?"

"I asked—"

"I heard you. I guess what I meant was, why would you ask such a thing?"

"Because I went to the feed store to see you and overheard your parents arguing over which one of them was to blame for your being pregnant."

She closed her eyes and turned around, then leaned back against her front fender.

"So it's true," he said, his voice going husky. "Maybe you've got the right idea." He stood next to her and leaned against her car, too. "I'm the father, aren't I."

She swallowed and nodded. "Yes."

Justin took three long, deep breaths and kept his jaw clenched to keep from bellowing at the top of his lungs. When he thought he could speak in a rational tone, he said, "This is why you've been avoiding me. You weren't going to tell me at all, were you?"

"Justin, I'm sorry." She turned toward him with a plea in her eyes. "I'm sorry. I panicked. I didn't know what to do. I'm still not sure. But I think when I figured things out, I would have told you about the baby."

Justin shook his head. Dear God, he was going to be a father. "How long have you known?"

She glanced down at the ground and kicked a pebble with the toe of her cowboy boot. "Since the night we spent together."

"Aw, come on. You couldn't have known that soon."

"Okay. If you say so."

"Look, Blaire, this has taken me by surprise, and that's putting it mildly. We need to talk about it."

"There's nothing to talk about, Justin. We spent a wonderful night together, but you don't owe me anything. I don't want or need anything from you, I don't plan to make any demands of you. Don't trouble yourself about me one little bit. I'll be just fine. Now if you'll move your truck, I'd like to get back to work. Daddy's waiting on this part."

Justin stood there for a long moment, unable to move, unable to think. All he could do was stare at her and hope the air would keep moving in and out of his lungs without his help, because he wasn't capable of anything just then.

He was going to be a father. Blaire Harding carried his child. And she wanted nothing to do with him. Not one damn thing.

He turned around and climbed into his pickup and started the engine. The next thing he knew, he was parked at home in front of the barn without a single memory of the thirty-minute drive.

By the time Blaire drove the three blocks back to the feed store and home, she was shaking so hard she could barely get the car in Park.

She had hurt Justin. Not just today, but every time she hadn't returned his call or gone out with him when he asked or spoken to him when they happened to end up in the same place at the same time.

And she had hurt herself. This entire mess was no one's fault but hers. If she hadn't given in and gone out with him in the first place, she would never have ended up in bed with him and none of this would have happened.

But he was so ruggedly handsome, so devilishly charming, and he had intrigued her for so many years. What was a girl to do? How did she keep saying no to his invitations time after time when all she'd wanted in the world was to say yes?

Then, when she had given in and gone out with him a few times, she had given in big time and made love with him that night at the motel.

She'd known before that night was over that she carried his child. She should have handled everything differently from that point on. She should have told him at once that she didn't want to see him anymore instead of making up excuses, then avoiding his calls.

How childish of her. How cowardly.

But how was she to look him in the eye and tell him she didn't want to see him anymore, when it was a bald-faced lie? She wanted very much to see him again. But she knew that couldn't be. Not now, not ever.

With a heavy sigh, she grabbed the sack from the hardware store and climbed out of her car. She carried the part to her father, but he wasn't behind the counter. Both her parents, she found a moment later, were in her office, yelling at each other.

So what was new?

"There you are," her father snapped. "You get my part?"

"I did." She tossed him the sack. "I have a bone to pick with the two of you."

"Oh, do you, now?" her father said. "Going to take us to task, are you?"

"I don't appreciate your discussing my private, intimate business in front of customers."

"We would never—" her mother began.

"You did. Both of you. Just a little while ago. Justin Chisholm came in and overheard your argument. Thanks to you, he now knows I'm pregnant."

"He what?" her father demanded. "You mean he sneaked in here and eavesdropped on our private conversation?"

"I mean you were shouting at the top of your lungs at each other. He was coming back here looking for me and couldn't help but overhear."

"Wait a minute." Blaire's mother narrowed her eyes and tapped a manicured nail to her cheek. "Did you go out with him here a while back?"

Here it comes, Blaire thought. She wouldn't lie to her parents, because it would serve no purpose. "Yes," she said.

"Is he the sorry bastard who did this to you?"

Blaire arched her brow. "Only if you were a sorry bastard when you 'did this' to Mother."

"You watch your language, young lady," he snapped.

"Huh," Blaire said in disgust. "What you really want to know is if Justin is the father of my baby. The answer is yes. And now he knows about it."

"Well, then," her mother said cheerfully. "We better start planning the wedding. How soon do you think we can put it together?"

"There isn't going to be any wedding," Blaire said firmly.

"What do you mean?" her mother asked, shocked.

"Is that sorry scoundrel refusing to marry you? Well, don't you worry about that. I'll set him straight quick enough."

"You'll do no such thing." Blaire glared at her father. "You won't say a word to him, not a single word. Justin and I are *not* getting married, and that's the way I want it. And that's final."

Her father bent forward and got in her face. "Don't you be telling me what's final and what's not. I say that boy is gonna do right by you, and you're gonna let him."

"You think Justin and I should get married just because I'm pregnant?"

"What better reason is there?" her mother wanted to know.

"I don't know, and it sure worked well for the two of you, didn't it?" Blaire knew she was going too far, but this was one line she would not allow her parents to cross.

"Do you want the two of us to end up as miserable as the two of you?" she demanded, nursing her anger, feeding it. "You want us to wind up hating each other the way you do? Blame the child for every lousy thing that happens, the way you've always blamed me?"

"We have never blamed you for anything. You just mind what you say, young lady."

"Every time one of you gets unhappy with the other, you've always said that if it wasn't for me you wouldn't have had to get married and none of this— whatever is happening at the moment, anything from plumbing leaks to hurt feelings—none of it would be happening if it wasn't for me. Is that what you want? You want your grandchild raised feeling like an albatross around her parents' neck?"

Her parents stared at her, speechless.

"What?" she demanded. "Did you think I haven't noticed, from the time I was old enough to understand the word *blame?* Don't try to tell me you never meant to make me feel this way, because this is exactly how you meant to make me feel. Responsible, to blame, for every bad thing that's ever happened in your life."

"Blaire, honey," her mother began.

"Don't, Mama. Just don't say anything. I am not going to marry a man I don't love, who doesn't love me, and that's final. The two of you are going to stay completely out of this, out of my business. If you don't, if you start meddling, I'll leave and disappear and I won't come back. And that's a promise."

"Well, now," her father said. "I think you're being stupid."

"We only want what's best for you and the baby," her mother said.

"Do you think it's best for this baby or any other to have two parents who can't stand to be in the same room together? Who fight all the time and don't care what hurtful words they use in front of the child? Is that what you think is best for me and the baby?"

Chapter Three

"Where are you going?" Sloan asked Justin. "I thought you were going to help me work on this tractor."

"You don't need me for that," Justin said. He needed something physical to do. Something hard and sweaty that didn't require thought or care. "Cattle and horses will need more hay by tomorrow. Thought I'd go load the hay trailer."

"If you ask me," Sloan said, tossing a wrench into the toolbox and fishing out a smaller one. "I'd guess you'd probably rather have hemorrhoids."

"Than load hay? I don't mind loading hay."

"Than have woman trouble. Which is what I figure you've got."

"You figure that, do you?"

"I do. Now I'm trying to figure out which woman it is who's got you so tied up in knots."

Justin wanted, badly, to pour it all out to big brother and let Sloan tell him what to do next, how to handle the situation. But he was a grown man, and this was an intensely private matter for him and Blaire. He figured he was going to need some advice along the way, but right now he needed to keep things between him and Blaire. It wasn't fair to go around revealing her condition before she was ready for people to know.

He shook his head at Sloan. "I'm not ready to say just yet, but I will be before long. Just let it be for now, okay?"

"Is it serious?"

"As a heart attack."

Sloan studied his younger brother for a long moment, then decided he could either browbeat the kid until he spilled his guts, or he could keep his mouth shut—which for a caretaker like himself was extremely difficult—and let Justin run his own life.

He gave a slow nod.

Justin returned the gesture and turned to go.

"Justin?"

Justin stopped but didn't look back. "Yeah?"

"I'm always here, whenever you're ready to talk."

Justin looked over his shoulder at the man who had been both father and brother to him all his life, even though there were only seven years separating them. "I know, Sloan. Thanks."

There was something therapeutic about hefting one sixty-five pound bale of hay after another and slinging it onto the trailer. Usually. It was a handy chore to tackle when a man needed to work off a mad, or a little extra energy.

Today it wasn't working. With every bale he lifted and tossed, he got madder. He had long since shed his coat, and now his shirt was getting damp. He'd worked up such a head of steam that the only way he knew the temperature was dropping was by the white cloud formed by each breath he huffed out.

If he was going to talk to Blaire again—and he damn well was—he'd better get this anger, this sense of betrayal under control.

He would like to say that she was the only one he was mad at, but it took two to make a baby, and he was the other half of this pair. If there was blame to be passed around, then it belonged to both of them. They'd even used a condom, both times. But condoms didn't come with a guarantee, or the makers would go broke paying child support for millions of children.

That Blaire was pregnant was not what angered him. He couldn't be angry about a child of his own making. But he could be and was angry that she knew and hadn't told him. From all indications, she'd had no plans to tell him any time in the near future.

He tossed another bale then, shoulders aching from not pacing himself, he sat on the fender of the trailer.

If he looked at the situation from Blaire's viewpoint—at least the best he could, considering that it wasn't his body that was invaded, which would now grow all out of shape and make him sick and maybe leave scars and let's not even think about the agony of childbirth.

Okay, so he couldn't get a good grasp on her viewpoint. But he could guess that she might be upset about suddenly finding herself pregnant when she hadn't planned to be. It might take a little getting used to.

Then, too, she would have to make certain she really was pregnant. They sold those test kits at every drugstore, grocery, and discount store in the country. Then maybe a visit to a doctor to confirm.

Justin had no idea what such a visit might entail, but he was pretty sure that it wasn't a barrel of laughs unless a woman was eagerly looking forward to the good news of an impending blessed event.

He didn't imagine Blaire had been any too eager to learn she was about to become a mother.

Justin had known her, although not well, for years. He'd been trying to get to know her better since last summer when she came back to town. He'd finally got her to go out with him, but only a couple of times before that night they'd spent together. Now she was carrying his child. She obviously was not happy about having this tie to him.

What a kicker, he thought. She was gorgeous, smart, sexy, and she was carrying his child. And she wanted nothing to do with him.

It was that last part that had him grinding his teeth and tossing hay bales.

Maybe it was just going to be too bad if she wanted nothing to do with him. She was going to need help throughout her pregnancy, and certainly after that. Financial help, emotional support, physical aid.

As the father of her child it was his duty—his *right*—to provide that help. She might throw it in his face, but one of the things he liked about her was her intelligence. She wasn't stupid enough to turn down needed help. Unless her pride got in her way.

The next day he decided to find out. He drove to the feed store, determined to see her and talk to her.

First, he had to get through her father.

"You!" At the first sight of Justin, Thomas Harding vacated his stool behind the counter so fast that it clattered to the floor. "What are you doing here?"

Justin did his best to put out of his mind the fact that Harding kept a loaded shotgun behind the counter. "Mr. Harding." Justin nodded. "I came to see Blaire."

"Hmph. Way I hear it," he said, something akin to hatred in his eyes, "you've *seen* more than enough of my little girl."

Justin swallowed. "She told you."

"She told us. You're gonna do the right thing by her, Chisholm. I mean to see to that."

"Whatever she wants, whatever she needs," Justin said. "That's why I'm here." *Whether she wants me here or not.* "Is she in the office?"

"Yeah, but not for long. If you wanna catch her you better get back there. And when you've seen her, you and I have some more talking to do, boy."

"Yessir, Mr. Harding. I imagine we do."

"In fact," Harding said as he started around the end of the counter toward Justin, "I think maybe we better do our talking right now, you and me." The gleam in the man's eyes promised retribution for the wrongs done to his daughter.

Justin held up both hands. "Now look, Mr. Harding—"

The bell over the front door jingled, announcing the arrival of more customers.

Harding stepped back behind the counter. "Go on," he said to Justin. "I'll get to you later."

How clichéd was that? Justin wondered. He'd just been saved by the bell.

As he stepped toward the side door that led to the office behind the outer room, Mr. Harding mumbled something he couldn't quite catch. It sounded a little like, "Keep your pants zipped."

Justin halted and looked back. "Sir?"

Mr. Harding scowled. "It's a little like closing the

barn door after the horse is out," he hissed quietly so the two customers at the other end of the room wouldn't hear, "but keep your…hands to yourself around my daughter."

Justin figured Blaire knew where she did and didn't want him to put his hands, but he didn't think her daddy would take too kindly to hearing that, so Justin merely nodded and went on his way.

At the door to the office, he stopped. "What the hell?"

Boxes were everywhere, on the desk, the chair, stacked on the floor. Boxes of file folders, office supplies and equipment, supply catalogs. It appeared that everything in the office was being crammed into boxes.

Blaire was on her knees emptying out a bottom file drawer and evidently had not heard him.

"Going somewhere?" he asked.

Blaire let out a squeak and slapped a hand over her heart. "You scared the daylights out of me."

"I'm sorry. I didn't mean to. I guess you were concentrating on what you're doing. What are you doing?"

She flapped her arms out, toward the boxes on either side of her. "What's it look like?"

"It looks like you're moving the office."

"You got it in one."

"Where to?"

"To my old room in my parents' house."

He looked around the cramped space, which had been added on years ago for office space. "You don't like it here anymore?"

She sighed and rose to her feet. "Why are you here, Justin?"

"I came to talk to you."

"I told you yesterday, I don't want or need anything from you."

"I know you did. I happened to disagree. I think we should talk about it."

She sighed again and rubbed her forehead. "I'm moving the office to the house because I don't think the pesticide and herbicide fumes in this place are good for the baby."

Her answer gave him pause. He'd been right that she was going to need help. This was one of what would probably turn out to be dozens of changes she would undergo during the coming weeks and months.

"I'm sure you're right," he told her. "Are any of these boxes ready?"

She looked at him with suspicion. "Why?"

He rolled his eyes. "So I can set fire to them. So I can carry a load over for you."

"I can't ask you to do that."

"As far as I'm concerned you could have. For that matter, I think you should have. But you didn't. I volunteered. I'll go get the two-wheeled cart."

"Why?" she asked.

"Why what?"

"I told you yesterday I didn't want or need anything from you. Why are you here offering help?"

"Why are you afraid of accepting it?"

Her spine stiffened as if someone had replaced it with a steel rod. "I'm not afraid."

"Fine." But he could see in her eyes that she wasn't sure if her statement was truth, or merely wishful thinking. "Then there's no reason not to accept my help. If it worries you, pretend I'm just the hired help. Back in a minute."

He turned and walked out before she could comment. She wanted to send him packing. He could read that much in her eyes. If he could get her to talk to him, trust him, maybe she would tell him why.

He found the two-wheeled cart in the giant storeroom next to the loading dock. How many times had he backed up to that very dock and helped one of Harding's employees, or Harding himself, stack a load of feed in his truck bed? Too many to count.

Now here he was, manning the cart himself so that the mother of his unborn child could get away from the fumes that lingered in every feed store he'd ever been in.

Blaire's father watched Justin's every move with a jaundiced eye.

Blaire herself watched Justin with almost as much distrust, but her look was tempered with a touch of curiosity. She wasn't sure what he was about. And that was fine with Justin. Better her uncertain curiosity rather than a more negative reaction.

He stacked boxes to the top of the handles on the cart, then followed Blaire as she led the way out into the storage room, down the loading ramp, and across the gravel drive to her parents' two-bedroom red-brick house twenty yards behind the store.

Mrs. Harding held the door open for them and offered Justin a tentative smile. So far she was the only member of the Harding family who didn't seem eager to see the last of him.

"It'll be a tight fit turning into the hall," she offered, "but we got a triple dresser in there, so these boxes should go all right."

With a little back-and-forth maneuvering of the two-wheeled cart, he got the boxes to the front bedroom with no trouble.

The room had been stripped of everything except the blinds on the windows. He eyeballed the space and had his doubts about its adequacy.

"Are your desk and file cabinets going to fit in here?" he asked.

"No," she said. "We'd never get that big desk of mine through the bedroom door. I'm going to work off a folding table for now, until we figure out something else."

"Did you consider using the garage?" he asked.

"Yes, but we'd have to pipe in heat and air and put

a wall up in place of the big door. This is only temporary, anyway."

"Is it?" he asked.

Blaire frowned at him. "You think I'm going to be pregnant the rest of my life?"

"No, but if breathing those fumes is not healthy for the baby, it can't be healthy for an adult, either, even if a baby's not involved."

Blaire's mother patted Justin on the arm, but she spoke to Blaire. "You picked a smart one, honey. He makes good sense."

Justin could see the muscle flex in Blaire's jaw as she obviously ground her back teeth together. "I haven't *picked* anybody for anything, mother, so just stop it right now."

"Now, honey, is that any way to talk about Justin?"

An explosion was definitely in the making, if the fire in Blaire's golden brown eyes was any indication. Since he was, in this case, a coward, and didn't want to witness a daughter annihilating her mother, or vice versa, he threw himself into the breach.

"It's all right, Mrs. Harding." He leaned down and whispered loudly, so Blaire would have no trouble hearing. "She's not too happy with me right now. I'd just as soon give her a little time to get over that."

Mrs. Harding's eyes twinkled with delight. She whispered back. "Flowers."

"No kidding?"

"A girl can never get too many flowers," Mrs. Harding confirmed.

"I'll remember that."

Blaire rolled her eyes and headed out the door, leaving Justin and her mother behind. "You'll be wasting your money," she muttered.

"It's my money to waste," he called after her.

Mrs. Harding winked at him. "Let's get these boxes unloaded so you can go after her."

"Yes, ma'am."

He caught up with Blaire just as she stepped back into her office. "What's next?" he asked, looking around. "How about a file cabinet or two?"

"Too much trouble. I can work out of boxes."

"For the next year? Why?"

"Justin." She heaved a sigh and shook her head. "Go home."

"I don't think so. I think I'll just wheel this empty file cabinet over to your new office."

"Justin."

He tilted the file cabinet to one side and slid the two-wheeler beneath it. In a matter of minutes he had it standing pretty as you please in her old bedroom at the end of the driveway.

"Oh, thank you," Mrs. Harding said. "That will make things so much easier on her. She's so stubborn, that girl of mine."

Since Blaire had refused to accompany him with the file cabinet, since she thought it was merely a nuisance to move it now, then have to move it back in a matter of months, Justin felt free to gather all the info he could about this woman who carried his child.

"Stubborn, is she?"

"Oh, my, yes. And smart. Don't you think she's not smart."

"No, ma'am. I know she's smart. That's one of the things I like the most about her."

"Justin Chisholm, you're playing me like a fish, and don't think I don't know it. If you want to know something about my girl, you just ask me. Better yet, ask her."

"I plan to ask her, but first I have to get her to talk to me. I'm working on that, too, since she thinks she doesn't need anything from me."

"That's pretty much what she thinks, all right."

"I better get back over there," he said with a nod to the store, "before she sneaks out and I have to chase her all over town."

Mrs. Harding tilted her head and studied him. "Yes," she said thoughtfully, "I think you would do just that, wouldn't you."

"Of course. Oh, and by the way. If I was playing you, it was more like a fine violin rather than a fish on the line."

Mrs. Harding threw her head back and laughed. "You go on now, and find my daughter. Make an honest woman out of her, see that you do."

Justin made no comment, just wheeled his cart

down the sidewalk and up the gravel drive. How was he supposed to make an honest woman out of a woman who didn't want him around?

Besides, to his way of thinking, there was nothing dishonest about her to begin with.

He found her standing in the middle of her torn up office with her hands on her hips, her back to the door, rolling her head back and forth as if to relieve an ache.

"Have you been overdoing it?" He parked the cart beside the door and crossed to her.

She whirled to face him. "You're back."

"I'm back." He put his hands on her shoulders and turned her around. "Here." He started massaging her neck and shoulders. "You're one big knot of muscles back here."

Blaire might have answered—surely would have thought of something coherent to say that would get him to stop touching her—but when she opened her mouth, all that came out was a low moan of pleasure and relief. His hands were magic. She should have remembered that about him. Had remembered, which might explain why she'd been so studious about keeping her distance from him.

She obviously wasn't very good at that particular task, keeping her distance. Here he was in her office. He'd just been in her parents' home twice, hauling her office stuff over there. Now he was giving her this mind-numbing massage that threatened to weaken her knees.

When he said, "Have dinner with me," she was incapable of saying no.

"Okay," she managed.

"Tomorrow night."

"Okay."

"I'll pick you up about six-thirty. Is that all right?"

"Um-hmm. Fine. No." She tore herself from his magic hands and whirled, staggering to catch her balance.

"What do you mean, no?"

Blaire swallowed. "I mean, I don't think we need to be having dinner together. There's no point in it."

"How about eating? That's a point. We both have to do it. Why not do it together?"

She shook her head. "There's more to it than that. You want something from me."

Slowly he nodded his head. "You're right. I want something from you. I want conversation. I want us to talk with each other. You need me, whether you think you do or not. I can help you. Let's talk about it and see if we can come up with a way to work things out that will satisfy both of us."

Blaire wanted to say no. Her pride and her fear wanted her to stand on her own two feet with no help from him or anyone else. But thousands of problems were staring her in the face and she wasn't sure she was up to handling them all on her own.

Maybe it was weak of her, but she finally agreed. "All right."

"Good," he said.

"I don't think there's any point to it, but all right. Dinner and talk. Nothing more."

"I'll see you at six-thirty."

She watched him go, wondering if she'd just made a serious mistake.

Chapter Four

Justin felt as nervous as a school boy on his first date. He couldn't remember the last time, even as a teenager, when he had tried on and discarded a half dozen shirts before deciding on one he liked. He would have said he was much too secure in his manhood, or some such self-affirming nonsense, except that the proof of his anxiety lay strewn across his bed.

He checked his watch. It was too early to leave.

He checked his hair. It was combed to within an inch of its life.

He checked his boots. Polished to a mirror-bright sheen.

He checked his jeans. The crease was straight and sharp. Thank you, Maria.

He exhaled into his cupped palm, but couldn't tell anything so popped a breath mint into his mouth for insurance.

Had he used deodorant? Yes, he had used deodorant, and he had on clean underwear, not that Blaire would know about the latter.

He was as ready as he would ever be.

He felt as if his entire future rested on this one single date. It probably wasn't true. If he didn't make any headway tonight on getting her to trust him, surely he would get another chance. By his calculations, he had seven months until his child—their child—was born to make certain that he would be a part of the child's life.

But more than that was going on here. He wanted to be part of Blaire's life, too. He just didn't know how large a part or how it would work. They had a great deal to talk about.

And if he kept thinking about it he would end up being late to pick her up.

He wasn't late. He parked his truck and climbed the stairs to her garage apartment at precisely 6:30 p.m.

When he knocked on the door, nerves had him knocking harder than necessary.

Inside the apartment Blaire flinched at the sudden pounding. She pressed a hand to her stomach and took a final glance in the mirror. He hadn't said where they were going, so if he'd intended someplace fancy, it would be his fault that they couldn't go. She had opted to wear jeans. She didn't want to go anywhere fancy. In Rose Rock, a person could eat anywhere, order anything from a corn dog to pizza to a giant, juicy sirloin and not be out of place wearing jeans. She wanted to wear hers as often as possible before she outgrew them in the coming weeks.

With a final nod and a brief prayer that she wasn't making a terrible mistake in going out with Justin, she left her room and went to answer the door.

"Hi," he said.

It was impossible not to return his smile. "Thank you for the flowers." He'd sent her an arrangement of daisies in a decorative coffee mug, with a note wishing her well in her new office. It was cute and thoughtful, even if it had been at her mother's prodding.

"You're welcome," he said. "I generally try to take a mother's advice on these things."

Blaire smirked, her bubble of good humor bursting. "You mean when she's trying to help you soften up her daughter?"

"Absolutely. I'm just grateful to have at least one person on my side around here. Not that I think there should be sides," he added quickly.

"But there apparently are," she stated. "Do you still want to eat?"

"I want to spend some time with you. It happens to be dinnertime. I haven't eaten, and I doubt you have, either. So, yes, I still want to eat. How about you?"

Her stomach chose that moment to growl. She blushed and realized that any answer other than yes would be laughable now.

"Let me get my purse and coat."

She pulled on her coat and grabbed her purse, then stepped out her door with Justin. He pulled her door closed behind them and made sure it was locked.

The stairs were not wide enough for them to walk side by side, so Justin motioned for her to go first.

"No, wait," he said. "I'll go first." He moved around her and took the first step down.

"Well, that was rude," she said to the back of his head.

"No," he said, pausing to look over his shoulder at her. "It's called chivalry."

"Excuse me? I thought it was always ladies first."

"Normally, yes," he admitted. "But think about it. A man is supposed to walk on the outside when a couple is walking down the street. That's to protect her from getting splashed, or from some ruffian accosting them."

"Ruffian?"

"Humor me. It's all about the man protecting the woman. How can I protect you from falling down the stairs if I'm behind you?"

"What, you think I can't manage the stairs without help? I'm pregnant, not incapacitated. Who's supposed to protect me the other dozen times a day

I go up and down these stairs? Or am I supposed to wait for some man—maybe you?—to come along and help me?"

"I was thinking of your safety," he said with what sounded like strained patience. "Are we really going to stand here and argue about who goes down the stairs first?"

When he put it that way, it sounded foolish. "I'd rather not."

"Are we both idiots?" His lips were quirking.

Her own twitched once or twice. "I can blame it on hormone imbalance. What's your excuse?"

He smiled at her. "Hunger."

He stood to the side and allowed her to pass and descend ahead of him. At his pickup he opened the passenger door for her and offered her a hand to give her a boost. It was a high step up into the cab.

When he pulled out onto Main Street, he turned away from town and headed the other way.

"Where are we going?"

"How does Mexican food sound? I thought I remembered hearing you say you liked it."

"I do. So, where are we going?"

"Norman."

Blaire blinked in the dimly lit cab. "But that's thirty miles away."

"Is that a problem? I promise not to make you walk home."

Maybe he wouldn't, she thought. But it certainly

took away her option to walk home if she wanted to. Why would he pick someplace so far, unless he had something sneaky in mind?

"You do remember that we agreed on dinner only. Nothing else."

"Dinner and conversation," he said. "You don't trust me enough to believe I mean it?"

"As crazy as it sounds under the circumstances, I really don't know you all that well, do I?"

He let the country music from the dashboard radio fill the cab for a long moment before he answered. "You trusted me well enough a couple of months ago."

"Don't take offense," she told him, "but that wasn't trust, it was foolishness."

"Ouch."

"Oh, I think your ego is tough enough to take it."

"You don't know me well enough to know that, do you?"

She chuckled. "Okay, I had that coming. Sorry. All of this, us, you and me, just feels a little awkward, you know?"

"You mean because of the baby?"

"You don't seem at all uncomfortable talking about it."

"I'm not uncomfortable about it," he admitted. "It wasn't something either of us planned. In fact, we took steps to prevent it, but they didn't work. It happened, and here we are. Now we have to deal with the situation the best way we can."

"And how might that be?" She would dearly love to know how this was supposed to work, this pregnancy, this parenthood that she did not feel at all prepared for.

"Well, first you go out to dinner with me and we maybe get to know each other a little better. Maybe, if we're lucky, we can be friends."

She swallowed. "Friends? Is that what you want?"

"I think it's a good place to start. Look," he said. "I know you said you don't need or want anything from me. Maybe you don't, but I think you will. Need, at least. I want us to be friends so that if you do need something, you'll feel comfortable enough with me to ask for it."

This time she was the one who was quiet for several minutes. "You've put a lot of thought into this."

"Not as much as you have, I'm sure, since I only found out yesterday."

That, she felt, was a criticism of her, for not telling him sooner about the baby. She would give him that one, because she felt guilty for having kept quiet once she'd had her pregnancy confirmed.

But how was a woman supposed to tell a man she'd been out with only a few times that she carried his child? *Oh, excuse me, but remember that night at the motel?*

She hadn't been up to the challenge of telling him. That would have to stop. She had a child on the way. She couldn't afford to chicken out on things anymore. She had to take charge, first of her own life, then of her child's.

He said he wanted to be friends. She could offer him that, couldn't she? Perhaps polite acquaintances would do. It wasn't her job to provide him with what he wanted. She had to look out for herself and the baby.

"By the way," he said, breaking into her thoughts. "Something I've been meaning to ask you."

"What's that?"

"Yesterday at the feed store, when I overheard your parents talking about…you and the baby and all, your mother said something about you knowing about the baby because your watch quit, or some such nonsense. Your dad seemed to know what that meant. What was she talking about?"

In the darkness of the cab, Blaire felt her left wrist, where she used to wear her watch. "My watch quit," she told him. "That night we spent together. It stopped running right after the first time we…had sex."

"Made love."

"Whatever."

"Made love," he insisted. "Had sex sounds too impersonal for what we shared. So your watch stopped. It happens."

"Yes. It happens to the women in our family, my mother, and my grandmother before her. And now me. When we conceive, something weird happens to our body's electricity or electrical current or whatever, and a watch won't run when we wear it on our wrist. My grandmother swears the antique watch she wore on a chain around her neck wouldn't run."

"You don't believe that, do you?"

"I have to."

"Maybe being pregnant makes you forgetful, so you don't remember to wind the watch," he offered.

"O ye of little faith. You probably don't remember, but I put your watch on that night for a few minutes, after mine quit running. When you put yours back on when we left, it was a few minutes slow. It quit while I wore it."

"The battery probably needs replacing."

"Mmm," was all she said.

"Look," he said. "You can't tell you're pregnant by whether or not your watch keeps time."

"It was verified with a few home test kits, and a follow-up visit to my doctor. I'm not making it up, Justin."

"I never thought you were. It's just, I don't know, weird. The watch thing, I mean."

"You're telling me. Now I never know what time it is, and I'm a person who likes to know."

"How about if I get you a new watch?"

"That would be nice, but it won't keep time on my wrist until after the baby is born."

"You're not serious."

"That's what I've been saying. From conception to birth, a watch isn't going to work on my arm.

Don't ask me to explain it. That's just the way it is. The same thing happened to my mother, and to her mother. Feel free to ask them."

"No, no. I believe you. I think."

They fell silent for a time, and Blaire wallowed around in her own thoughts, buried so deep in them that she didn't notice when he left the interstate and hit city traffic. Then he was pulling into a parking lot at the restaurant. It was the sudden silence from his killing the engine and cutting off the radio that finally got her attention.

"Earth to Blaire," he said, waving a hand before her face.

Embarrassed, she offered a smile. "Sorry. I was lost in thought."

"Well, come on, let's go get lost in enchiladas."

Before she could gather her purse from the seat beside her and reach for the door handle, he was out of the pickup, around the hood and opening her door for her. Playing the gentleman again.

She wondered how hard he had to remind himself to do the gentlemanly thing, or if it came naturally.

From what she knew of the way he and his brothers were raised, by their grandmother, Blaire thought maybe such behavior might be ingrained in them. Cherokee Rose Chisholm was a legend in the state of Oklahoma. She was known for her strength of character, her integrity and her livestock.

Blaire wondered what the woman would have to

say about the feed-store owner's daughter ending up pregnant by her youngest grandson.

She wondered if the woman already knew.

She wasn't ready to face Rose Chisholm. Good heavens, she could barely face herself in the mirror each morning. Facing her parents had been a nightmare, Justin almost that bad. But facing Justin's family? No way. She couldn't do it. Not yet.

So much for her bravery, she thought as they stepped into the blasting warmth and rolling noise of the restaurant.

The food was hot and spicy, just the way Blaire liked it. The restaurant was crowded, the music loud and fast. The decor consisted of sombreros, serapes and piñatas. It was not an atmosphere for relaxing.

Justin had picked this restaurant deliberately so that Blaire wouldn't think he was trying to seduce her, which, under other circumstances, he would most certainly do.

But in order to have any chance at a conversation, he had to sit next to her rather than across from her, and that raised her eyebrows.

"I just want to be able to talk," he said, leaning toward her. "Without us having to yell at each other."

"I didn't say anything."

"Your eyes did," he told her.

"If you're going to read my eyes, then I don't need to talk at all."

"I don't remember you being this perverse."

"Like I said," she told him with a wry smile. "We don't really know each other."

"Oh, I know what that means. It means you were on your best behavior when we dated, and now this is the real you."

For an instant she looked startled, telling him he'd hit close to home with his comment.

"I'm sorry," he said quickly. "Forget I said that. You're right. We don't know each other well enough. My favorite flower is the pansy. What's yours?"

Blaire blinked, then stared at him. "What?"

"Your favorite flower. What is it?"

"You're crazy, you know that?"

"I've been called that a time or two, but you don't need to worry. I don't think it's genetic."

She chuckled for a moment, then frowned. "Is there anything genetic I should know about?"

Justin twisted his head sideways, hunched one shoulder, and let his tongue hang out the side of his mouth. "Like what?" he asked.

She laughed.

He loved hearing her laugh. He didn't mind making a fool of himself if it made the tension and nerves fade from her eyes.

"As far as I know," he said, straightening up, "there's nothing genetic from my family that should cause a problem. The kid will be part Cherokee, of course. I assume that's no problem."

She pursed her lips. "If it was, we wouldn't be in this situation, would we?"

"Good point. So maybe you don't have a favorite flower. What's your favorite color?"

She shook her head. "You really are crazy."

"You said we didn't know each other. I'm trying to fix that. Come on. Give."

She rolled her eyes. "All right. Purple."

"Now we're making progress. It's mine, too." He rubbed his hands together. "Here's something we never talked about before. Why didn't we ever know each other in school? I'm only three years older than you. As small as Rose Rock is, seems to me we should have run into each other a long time ago instead of just the last year or two."

"We really are strangers, aren't we?" she said. "We didn't move to town until I was a junior. You would have graduated by then."

"That's right," Justin said. "I remember when your dad bought the feed store. How did I miss seeing you there?"

"I don't know. I remember seeing you."

The news surprised him. "Do you, now?"

"I do."

Those words…. They rang over and over in his head. Something about them filled him with both anticipation and apprehension.

"I bet things have changed a lot out at your ranch since both your brothers have gotten married in the past few months."

"Yes and no," he said. "The work hasn't changed, it's just been redistributed. We've taken on another hand, and Sloan and I have taken on more work, since Caleb's over at the Pruitt Ranch now. Plus we have Pedro. He takes up some of the slack, too. And he does a lot of the things that just weren't getting done. But the house, now that's different."

"You mean without Caleb?"

"Yeah, and with all the females." He grinned. "We've got Emily and her two girls, Libby and Janie. And then there's Maria, our new housekeeper, and her little baby Rosa. A man can't turn around anymore without running into a female. And no, ma'am, that is not a complaint."

"You like women."

"All ages, all kinds. I just like people. Don't you?"

She munched on a salsa-dipped chip and thought for a moment. "Not particularly. I guess I'm most comfortable with my own company."

"Nothing wrong with that," he said. "In fact, as much as I love my family, I've had my eye on one particular spot on the far side of the ranch where I'd like to build a house of my own."

"And not live with your family?"

"This would be for a family of my own, eventually. It's a little spot along a side road that doesn't get much traffic. I'd build a house right between an old buffalo wallow and this little persimmon grove where the deer come in the fall to eat the ripened fruit."

"For their sake, I hope they wait until it's truly ripe."

Justin laughed. "No kidding. You ever taste a green persimmon?"

She puckered her lips and made a face.

He laughed again. "You must have had Mr. Bollinger for Biology."

"Yes, and it was hideous. That man should be shot for making us all take a bite from one of those things. I bet I walked around school with my mouth all puckered up for hours afterward."

"You and me both," he said with a shudder. "I've never tasted anything so sour before or since. Did he laugh at your class the way he did us?"

"Like we were all idiots for doing what he told us?"

"Yep."

"Yes," she said, laughing. "He did."

They took their time with the meal, enjoying the food, the atmosphere, and, Blaire had to admit, the company.

Oh, she had certainly enjoyed his company in the past. That much was impossible to deny. But from what she saw of the world, once a guy got what he wanted out of a girl, he had no more use for her. It was time to move along in search of fresh game.

Such a thing had never happened to her, but she'd

seen her friends and cousins treated that way time and again. She had no particular reason to trust men.

"Even if you didn't move to town until I was out of high school," Justin said as if the conversation had never lulled. "Why didn't I know you until the past couple of years? Mostly the past few months, really, unless you count the few weeks you were in town summer before last, and now and then at holidays."

She arched a brow. "Been keeping tabs on me?" The idea thrilled her.

"Now and then," he offered with a grin. "Why didn't I know you better before this summer?"

"Probably because I went away to college right after high school. I got my teaching degree and a job teaching in Oklahoma City."

"But you're not teaching here, are you? In Rose Rock?"

"No." She shook her head and pushed the last few grains of refried rice around on her plate. "No, last June my mother fell and broke her arm. It was pretty bad. It took three surgeries to fix it. I came home to take over the office at the feed store for her and daddy. But she wasn't well enough by the end of summer for me to leave, so I had to stay."

"Will you be able to get your job back next year?"

She shook her head. "They've already said no."

"Because of all the budget cuts statewide."

"You got it in one try."

"Do you miss teaching?

"Like I imagine you would miss your favorite horse."

He winced. "That much, huh?"

"That much. But I'll get over it. We do what has to be done, right? I'll teach again someday."

Justin decided they had tiptoed around the subject *du jour* long enough. He took a deep breath and dived in. "It's not going to be easy being a single mother."

"Believe me," she said with feeling. "No one is more aware of that than I am."

"You don't have to do it alone, you know."

"I think the term 'single parent' indicates one is parenting alone."

"I mean," he said with a quick smile, "that you don't have to be a single parent."

She looked at him warily. "What—no. No way. Don't even—"

"Hear me out," he said before she got any further in her rejection. "Just think about it, will you?"

"Think about what?"

"About you and me getting married."

She pushed back in her chair and made ready to rise. "You're out of your mind."

"I am not. It's a good idea, if you'll just give it a chance."

"Why on earth would you think it's a good idea, when we've been agreeing all night that we barely know each other?"

"I want my child to carry my name and not be a bastard."

She opened her mouth to retort, then shut it before saying anything.

He had to give her credit for that. But he would add more to the deal, to tempt her. "You wouldn't have to work at the feed store or anywhere else if you didn't want to. You wouldn't have to worry about money or health insurance or a place to live or climbing up and down those damn stairs to your apartment when you're nine months along. Unless you wanted us to live there together after we're married."

She stared at him as though he'd suddenly grown a wart in the middle of his nose.

"Is it my words you don't understand?" he asked, "or my meaning?"

"You really are out of your mind. Of course I'm not going to marry—"

"Wait." He stopped her before she could finish. "Don't answer me yet. Think about it. Will you? Please? Just think about it. We like each other well enough, and I'm pretty easy to get along with. If it doesn't work out, at least we should be able to hold it together long enough to get you and the baby on your feet, so to speak. Unless you want me to raise the baby."

"What?"

"I said—"

"Hell and damnation, I heard you! You can just get

that thought out of your mind right this minute, Justin Chisholm. Nobody's raising this baby but me."

"I didn't know, wasn't sure how you felt about it."

"How I felt?" she nearly shrieked. "How do you think I feel?"

"I don't know. You've acknowledged that you're carrying my child, but you've never indicated whether or not you want the baby."

She crossed her forearms protectively over her abdomen. "Not want it? How can I not want my own baby?"

"Because you don't know me very well? Because you don't trust me at all? Because being a single parent doesn't fit in with your plans? A lot of women aren't too happy to end up in your shoes."

"I'm not a lot of women," she said hotly. "I would never give my child over to someone else to raise."

He was starting to get a little steamed himself. "You say that like I'm some bum on the street. Like having me raise him would be like giving him to some stranger. I'm not 'someone.' I'm the baby's father."

"You think I can't be a good mother? Is that it?"

"No, that's not it," he denied. "Of course that's not it. If we get married we won't have to argue over who raises the baby. We'll both raise him."

"Or her."

"Or her. Just think about it. Don't say no right off. Think about all the advantages. Sleep on it tonight, and I'll call you tomorrow. If you need more time than that, just say so, but I'll call you tomorrow anyway."

Blaire wanted to tell him not to bother, because there was no way on God's green earth she was going to marry a man who didn't love her, a man she didn't love, simply because doing so might make her life a little easier.

But she held her tongue. Still feeling guilty for his having to find out about the baby by accident, she felt she owed him. She would think about it.

She would say no, but she would think it through first.

She wasn't sure where she would find the nerve to look him in the eye and turn him down, but she would have to manage. If she couldn't do that, how did she think she could raise a child?

Chapter Five

Justin had told Blaire he would call her the next day. But when the next day arrived, he knew he couldn't simply call her on the phone. That would make it too easy for her to say no. He had to see her in person. To look into her eyes when she gave her answer.

Good God, he had asked a woman to marry him. He couldn't believe he was even remotely calm about it. Proposing marriage had not been in his plans when he'd picked Blaire up yesterday evening. At least, he hadn't consciously thought about it.

But as the evening wore on, the idea just sort of seeped in a little bit at a time until it was just...

there. A whole idea, as if it had always been there. Nothing startling or surprising or scary about it. Merely the most logical, practical thing for all concerned.

The few times in his life when he'd looked ahead and imagined himself married, logic and practicality had played no part in it. Nothing sounded more boring or deadly to him than a logical, practical marriage.

Wasn't there supposed to be love? Respect? Passion?

He and Blaire had the passion. Or they'd had it, a couple of months ago. But he couldn't imagine it not being there the next time he touched her. Last night he had deliberately kept his mind off such things, but the wanting had been there, under the surface, waiting to be let loose.

Respect? He respected what he knew of her. She'd gone to college, taught school, come to her parents' rescue when they'd needed help. She had sacrificed her job for them. And upon finding herself single and with an unplanned pregnancy, she was not demanding Justin marry her or support her or anything else.

There was a lot to respect in her.

But love? Justin had never been in love, so how would he know? There was no getting around the fact that she was right about them not knowing each other well.

They knew each other well enough to make a

baby, but then, that didn't take much knowing, outside the biblical definition of the word.

But he liked her. Liked her a great deal. They were good together, on the dance floor and in bed. They were both adults. Surely they could figure out a way to make a marriage work, even if they weren't madly in love. Maybe not having all that steamy emotion clouding the issue would be a benefit, helping them see their way more clearly.

He wanted to talk with her. If she hadn't made up her mind yet, maybe he could convince her. Because the one thing he knew beyond doubt was that he wanted to be a part of his child's life. No child of his was going to grow up without a father.

He wanted to talk with her, and he wanted to do it now.

But he couldn't walk out on Sloan when there was work to be done. It had been he, himself, who had mentioned that the livestock would need hay. He'd even loaded the trailer. It was time to distribute it.

And so they set out, he and Sloan, with Sloan driving the pickup, pulling the trailer Justin had loaded with hay. Creeping along like an arthritic turtle because there were no paved or gravel roads heading into the back pastures, only rough tire tracks left by countless trips just like this one.

Sloan was driving the best he could, trying to keep the pickup from bottoming out in the potholes.

"Can't you drive this thing any faster?"

"Oh," Sloan drawled slowly. "I probably could if I put my mind to it."

"Then do it, would you? Some people have other things to do today."

"Next time one of us runs out of things to do, we need to hook up the box blade and grade this damn road," Sloan said.

"Grade it so we can call it a road, you mean."

"Whatever. Anyway," he said, keeping the rig to the same slow, lumbering pace, "what's your hurry? The cattle and horses aren't likely to starve to death before we get to them."

It was all Justin could do to keep from bouncing his knee up and down. He hated doing that, because he hated it when other people did it around him. It indicated impatience with the current situation, a nervous desire to do something else. Made him feel…superfluous. Worse, in the way.

"No particular hurry," he said, forcing a slow, deep breath.

"How'd your date go last night? Who was the lucky lady?"

He was going to have to tell the family, and soon. They had a right to know that the youngest Chisholm was about to produce the youngest Chisholm.

Before he told them, however, he would warn Blaire of his intentions. She had a right to know that he was about to share their private news with his whole family.

"The date was fine. Mexican food up in Norman. I took Blaire."

"Blaire Harding? No fooling?"

"Why?"

Sloan shrugged. "I don't know. Seems like you've been hot after her for months. I remember you hooked up with her a couple of times a while back, but you haven't mentioned her in weeks. Are you two back on?"

"More or less. Maybe. We'll have to see."

It was the middle of the afternoon before Justin could legitimately shake loose and head to town. He didn't see Blaire's car in the driveway of the feed store parking lot, but he didn't worry about it. It could be in the garage.

He skipped the store and went straight to the house. Blaire's mother answered the door.

"Justin, hello. Come in." With a big smile, she stood back and motioned for him to enter.

"Thank you, ma'am."

"I think you better start calling me Nancy, don't you?"

"If you say so. Nancy. I'd like that."

"Me, too," she said, patting him on the arm.

"I came to see Blaire. Is she here?"

Nancy Harding's smile tightened. "Oh, dear. Well, to be completely honest, Justin…"

"Yes?"

"I'm sorry, but, no, she's not here."

"Oh, okay. I can go get a cup of coffee at the café or something. When do you expect her back?"

"I'm afraid she won't be back for a day or two. Maybe even a week."

Justin felt his gut clench. "Did something happen? Where'd she go?"

"You have to understand, Justin, she's under a great deal of stress these days."

"I do understand that. I offered her a partial solution to help her out, and we were supposed to talk about it today. You mean she just took off?"

"She went up to Enid to her cousin Connie's."

"Enid?" He blinked, dumbfounded. "She went to Enid?"

"That's right." Mrs. Harding—Nancy—turned her head and gave him a sly look from the corner of her eye. "I could give you the address, if you're interested. Something tells me you wouldn't get very far by calling her."

"Something tells me you're right," he muttered. "Okay, yes. I'll take that address. Thanks."

"I have it right here." She picked up a piece of paper from the end table near the door, as if she'd known he would come and would need the information.

"You're a peach, Mrs.—Nancy." He leaned down and brushed his lips across her cheek.

Blushing to beat the band, Nancy beamed at him.

"You go after my little girl, Justin, and you do right by her."

"I'm trying, ma'am. Nancy. I'm trying."

It was after dark by the time Justin reached Enid and located the address Nancy had given him.

He'd tried, very hard, to keep from losing his temper during the drive. First, because he tended to drive fast when he was angry, and second, he didn't want to jump to any erroneous conclusions regarding Blaire's sudden trip to Enid.

Maybe it wasn't a sudden trip. Maybe she'd had it planned.

But she hadn't said so, and her mother hadn't indicated such. He was inclined to believe that either this was Blaire's way of telling him she wasn't interested in marrying him, or she planned to tell him no, but couldn't face him. Or, he thought, she was running scared, not knowing what to do.

He hoped it wasn't the latter, because that would mean his offer of marriage had added more pressure than it had alleviated. Adding pressure to Blaire was the last thing he wanted to do.

The polite thing to do now would be to get a room for the night and come back to her cousin's house tomorrow, around midmorning.

But there was every chance that her mother would tell her he'd been by to see her and was coming to Enid. If Blaire would leave town knowing he was going to call, that he was expecting an answer to his proposal, such as it was, she would surely disappear on him this time, too.

He parked his pickup in the street and walked up the driveway, then the short sidewalk to the front door, where he rang the bell.

Behind the door a dog barked, a child shrieked and giggled.

A man about Justin's age opened the door with a wriggling, giggling toddler under one arm. "Yes?"

"I'm Justin Chisholm. I'm looking for Blaire Harding. Her mother said I'd find her here."

The man eyed Justin carefully. "Her mother sent you, you say?"

"Yes. Her mother. Is Blaire here?"

"Hey, Blaire," the man yelled over his shoulder.

"Annie Bare, Annie Bare," squealed the child.

"That's Aunty Blaire," the man explained. "I'm the local interpreter. Somebody here to see you," he added over his shoulder.

Blaire came through the doorway from the hall, wiping her hands on a dish towel. At the sight of Justin she stopped dead in her tracks. "Justin."

"Hi."

"What are you doing here? Go on, Billy, I'll handle this," she said to the man with the toddler under his arm.

"Are you sure?" he asked, eyeing the tight look on her face.

"I'm sure. It's fine. Go help Connie in the kitchen. She'd appreciate that, you know."

Billy rolled his eyes and hauled the kid down the hall.

Blaire rushed over to the door and practically pushed Justin back out onto the porch. It was cold enough that their breath came out in white puffs.

"What are you doing here?" she hissed.

Justin eyed her a minute and sucked on the inside of his jaw. "The more pertinent question, I'd say, is what are you doing here?"

"I came to see my cousin, if it's any of your business."

"Any of my business? Last night we talked about getting married."

"You talked about it."

"You said you would think about it. We agreed I was going to call you today for your answer. You're not home for me to call you, so here I am. Waiting for my answer." He wanted those last words back the instant they were out of his mouth. He had just as much as dared her to throw his suggestion of marriage back in his face.

Which was essentially what she did when she laughed. "You mean you were serious about that?"

If she thought she could hurt his feelings and send him running off with his tail between his legs, she was sadly mistaken. If she thought he was buying this casual woman-of-the-world act, she was deluding herself.

"I had no idea," she added.

Justin folded his arms across his chest and shifted his weight. "Bull hockey."

She laughed. "Bull what?"

"Hockey. I'm about to become a father in a few months. I'm cleaning up my language. Are you going to marry me, or do you need more convincing?"

Shaking her head, she held her palm out toward him and backed away until her back was to the door. "Justin, don't."

"Don't what? I realize it's a big decision, but don't you think sitting down and talking about it would be more productive than running away?"

She snapped straight, as if a drill sergeant had just called attention. "I wasn't running away."

"Sorry. My mistake." He moved in closer to her to shield her from the north wind. "But that's what it looks like from my view."

"I can't help what it looks like to you."

"Can't help, or don't care?"

She threw her hands in the air. "What do you want from me?" she cried. "I knew there was a reason I didn't tell you about the baby. You're just going to pester me to do things I don't want to do. I won't be pushed around, Justin. I won't be pressured."

"That's fair," he told her. "I don't make a habit of pushing people around, and I don't intend to start with you. If taking you to dinner puts pressure on you, I'm sorry. If asking you to marry me to give our child legitimacy and the Chisholm name puts pressure on you, I'm sorry. You won't be pushed around, I won't be brushed off or ignored."

"Hmph." She folded her arms across her chest. "Ignoring you would be about like trying to ignore a mountain lion in your living room."

"I don't know," he said, slipping off his leather bomber jacket and putting it around her shoulders. "You seem to be doing a pretty good job of it."

"Don't." She slid his jacket off and pushed it back into his hands. "I'm going back inside."

"All right. That's probably a good idea. I don't want you catching cold, and I don't want you blaming me if you do."

"Why would I blame you?"

"Because you're not too happy with me right now, I'm guessing."

"I don't like the idea of your following me all the way here."

"Why did you leave without telling me?"

She gave a toss of her head, but spoiled the gesture of defiance by sniffing and rubbing the end of her nose. "I don't answer to you."

"No, you don't answer to me. But I wish you would answer me about us getting married."

"All right, look. If you must know, I came up here so I could spend a couple of days not thinking about it."

He gave her a small smile. "I guess I ruined that, huh?"

"I guess you did." She shivered in an icy gust of wind.

Justin reached out and rubbed her arms, which were clad only in the thin cotton of her blouse. "Go inside before you freeze to death. I'll call you tomorrow."

She swallowed and looked at him a long moment, then nodded. "All right. But I don't think I'm going to be ready to talk about any of this tomorrow."

"I'll call you. You can tell me then if you're ready or not. Fair enough?"

She gave him a reluctant nod. "Fair enough."

Against his will, Justin stepped back and watched her go back into the house. The door closed softly but surely in his face.

On his way to find a motel room for the night, he tried to decide if he'd made a mistake in coming after her like this. There were no promises between them, no ties, other than the baby. She wasn't answerable to him or he to her.

But dammit, he wouldn't have left town knowing she expected to talk with him without letting her know he was going. She should have had the courtesy to at least tell him she didn't have an answer for him yet.

Instead, she had fled.

He knew she hadn't left him a message on his cell because he had checked. When he'd called home to tell them he wouldn't be home tonight he'd asked if there were any messages for him, and they'd said no.

He found a motel and checked in. The night passed slowly for him. He was tired, but his mind would not shut down. He kept remembering the last time he'd stayed in a motel. He hadn't slept that night, either. But that had been because he'd been too busy making love with Blaire Harding. Busy creating their child.

A baby. She was having his baby. The thought left him awed. As if no man in the world had ever sired a child before.

When Justin had left Blaire at her cousin's, Blaire had closed the door behind herself and leaned against it, closing her eyes for a moment to regain her mental balance.

She wondered if it was normal to feel like the only woman in the world to conceive a child outside of wedlock. Shouldn't she feel guilty? Ashamed?

She felt neither of those things.

Instead, this sharp sense of anticipation, mixed with enough nerves to keep her careful and attentive, permeated her from head to toe.

"Was that him?"

Blaire gave a start at the sound of Connie's voice a scant few inches away. In fact, she was right next to Blaire, peeking between the blinds on the living room window next to the front door.

"Wow." Connie let out a low whistle. "Looks like a keeper to me."

With a half snort, half laugh, Blaire gave her cousin and best friend a slight shove. "He's not a damn fish."

"Maybe not, but he still looks like a keeper to me. What's he like? Oh, never mind. Sit down first, before you fall down. He really gets to you, doesn't he?"

Sitting down seemed like the thing to do, so Blaire sat. It would have been too embarrassing to slide down the door and end up on the floor.

"What am I going to do, Connie?" Blaire buried her face in her hands and strove for calm. She could tell Connie anything.

There were four of them. They called themselves the Four Cousins. Or sometimes just The Four, or the Four Musketeers, or the Four Stooges. Whatever the occasion called for.

Connie, Sherry, Gayle and Blaire. They were all about the same age, and their mothers were sisters. The Four knew each other's secrets, heartaches, triumphs. And phone bills, because they called each other all the time and ran up ridiculous charges.

Connie rubbed Blaire's shoulder and made a humming sound in her throat. "What do you want to do?"

"I don't know. How am I supposed to know? I can't think straight around him. I can't even think straight about him. When I think about him or get near him my heart starts pounding, my palms sweat, my lungs don't want to work."

"You've got it bad, don't you."

"I guess I do, whatever *it* is. When I'm with him and all these stupid things are going on inside me, he can ask me a reasonable question and I get all defensive and stubborn and stupid, and I know he must think I'm an idiot, but I can't seem to help myself. What's wrong with me?" she wailed. "Is this what I have to look forward to until the baby comes? Is this what it's like to be pregnant? Raging hormones and all of that?"

Connie shook her head in commiseration. "That might be part of it, but what it really sounds like to me is something else entirely."

Alarmed, Blaire straightened and stared at her cousin. "Is it bad? Can it harm the baby?"

"It's only bad," Connie said, "if it's not reciprocated."

"What are you talking about?"

"I'm talking about love, dummy. You're in love with the guy."

"No." Blaire jumped up from the sofa and started pacing the length of the living room. "Oh, no. Absolutely not. It's impossible."

"Why? You must have felt something for him at one time." Connie got up and paced beside Blaire, bending over and peering up into Blaire's face. "I know you, cuz. If you hadn't cared a great deal about him, you never would have slept with him."

"That's beside the point. That's lust, not love."

"Um-hmm. Sure. Lust, that's fine. It's important. But it's not enough to get you to strip down and do the deed with a guy you've been out with only a few times. You know I'm right."

Blaire stopped pacing and made a face. "So what if you are right? So what if I felt something a couple of months ago? That doesn't mean I'm in love with the man. Feeling something and being in love are a mile apart."

"If you say so."

"Now you're humoring me."

"Hey. You asked my opinion, I gave it. If you want my advice, I say grab on to him with both hands and don't let go. He's a Chisholm, for crying out loud. From the Cherokee Rose. You can't do better than that. Those Chisholms have got honesty and integrity coming out their pores. I bet before another week goes by he asks you to marry him."

Blaire heaved a sigh. "He already did."

"What?"

Another sigh, this one of disgust. "You heard me. He asked me last night when he took me out to dinner. All the way to Norman, no less. He said he would call me today for my answer."

"Ah, now I see." Connie crossed her arms and tapped the fingers of one hand against the elbow of the opposite arm. "He was going to call you for an answer, so, logically, you got in your car and took off without giving him that answer. Good heavens, no wonder he drove all the way up here after you. The man wants to *marry* you!"

Blaire sat heavily on the sofa again and, with a groan, buried her face in her hands. "Only because he happened to accidentally get me pregnant. You know that doesn't work."

"Maybe it would. It could. He already likes you. Why wouldn't he fall in love with you? And what if he didn't? You could still—"

"Two words," Blaire said darkly. "My parents."

Connie stopped, nodded. "Okay. Fair enough. So what are you going to do? And you know, don't you, that just because your parents—"

"I know, I know, I'm not my parents. But I'd be a fool, wouldn't I, to ignore their lessons?"

A cry and a crash came from the kitchen.

"Oh, God. Billy. I left him alone in the kitchen."

"He's a grown man," Blaire protested. "Whatever it is, he can handle it."

"The last time he handled it, the fire department had to come put it out."

Blaire choked back a bark of laughter and followed her cousin into the kitchen to see what disaster Billy had created this time.

"Dammit, Billy!"

"'Ammit, Beeowy!" mimicked their toddler.

"Here." Connie plucked her son from his father's arms and handed him to Blaire. "Get him out of the line of fire. Or, in this case," she said with disgust, kicking at a clump of suds oozing out of the dish-washer, "the line of suds. It's going to get bloody in here. He's too young to witness what I'm about to do to his father."

With her lips mashed together to keep from laughing at the look of panic on Billy's face, Blaire hustled the youngster out of the kitchen.

Billy, it seemed, had used dish washing soap instead of dishwasher detergent in the dishwasher. An honest mistake—for an idiot—but for the fact that it wasn't the first time for Billy. He'd been positive that the last time had been a fluke, that Connie had just given him a hard time because she had to clean up his mess. After all, what did he know about mops?

He'd actually thought he could get away with it this time.

"And you think I need a husband?" Blaire cried in mock horror.

Connie laughed. "Oh, but he has his uses."

At ten o'clock Blaire hugged her cousin good-night and went to bed.

When the family arose the next morning, she was gone.

Chapter Six

"Gone?" *Count to ten, man. Be calm. Don't lose your temper,* Justin told himself. "What do you mean, she's gone?"

"Come in, come in." Connie took him by the arm and led him into her house. "Have a seat. Can I get you a cup of coffee?"

"No, thanks." She was gone. She had run out on him again. A smart man might start to get a certain message here. He blinked and looked around, not remembering how or why he was inside Blaire's cousin's house, seated on her gray and white sofa with a fuzzy kitten staring at him from the arm of the sofa and a stuffed purple dinosaur between his feet.

"Okay." Connie let out a hefty sigh. "I'm going to butt in where I don't belong."

Justin eyed her. "You are?"

"She's scared."

"Blaire? I think I got that."

"Two points for you, then. What are you going to do about it?"

He shook his head. "There's not much I can do but back off for now and try later to get close to her again."

Connie nodded and rocked back and forth in thought. "That might work. Eventually. Maybe by the kid's tenth birthday."

Justin stiffened.

"Yes, I know all about it. We're cousins, Blaire and me. Close cousins. There are four of us. We've been best friends since our mamas plunked us all in the same wading pool together before we were old enough to talk."

"Does that mean you have a suggestion?"

She thought for a moment, then gave a sharp nod. "Yes. My name's Connie, by the way. You need to go after her."

"If she's afraid of me, I'm going to come off looking like a stalker."

"It's not you she's afraid of. It's your feelings for her. It's her own feelings, her own judgment. She doesn't trust them. She's afraid of making a mistake that will hurt her and be bad for the baby."

Justin cocked his head and studied the woman before him. "I've never had the impression that Blaire was afraid of much of anything."

"Believe me, this is a biggie for her. She's normally the most self-confident woman I know. But marriage and babies, that's like her greatest fear."

"She's afraid of childbirth?" he asked sharply.

"No, no, I didn't mean it like that. She's afraid she won't do a good enough job and the baby will grow up unhappy or something."

"And why does she think that?" he asked.

Connie shook her head. "That's for her to tell you. I've said too much already. But I think you need to go after her, show her you're serious about getting married. You are serious, aren't you?"

"As a heart attack."

Connie grinned. "You're in love with her."

Justin jerked as if she'd slapped him. "Of course not. We barely know each other."

"Oh, yeah." Connie laughed. "Two peas in a pod. I expect an invitation to the wedding."

Within a few minutes Justin was on his way to Cousin Sherry's house in Ponca City, just over an hour away.

The sky was overcast and the temperature was dropping. He hoped that little old car of Blaire's was in good condition.

It was late morning when he pulled up at the apartment complex Connie had directed him to. Two minutes later he was knocking on the door to number 317.

A woman about Blaire's age, attractive with red hair and freckles, answered the door.

"Oh. Hello," she said. The look on her face said she had a good idea who he was.

"Hi. I'm Justin—"

"Chisholm."

"Right. Is Blaire here? I saw her car in the parking lot."

Cousin Sherry, if that's who this was, grinned at him. "Oops. There goes that excuse."

"Would you tell her that all I want is about a half hour of her time? I could take her for a late breakfast or early lunch, or just a cup of coffee. Someplace where the two of us can sit down and talk."

With a smile, the woman shook her head. "I'll tell her, but I doubt she'll go for it."

"Just tell her to quit cowering in the corner and come out and face me," he said with disgust. "She's acting like I'm the friendly local ax murderer. I'm just the guy who wants to marry her."

Sherry's mouth opened, then formed a round O. She blinked a couple of times. "Wow. I'll, uh, I'll just go, uh, get her."

"You can't just keep putting him off and running away," Sherry hissed at Blaire. "That man wants to marry you. You're having his baby. Forget your parents, dammit. Quit being so stubborn and go for it. You can always divorce him later. And think of the alimony."

"Sherry!" Blaire was appalled by the suggestion that she would want to live off alimony from Justin.

She refused to think about the first part of that, that the marriage could be temporary. At least, she tried to refuse it, but it somehow kept sneaking back into her thoughts.

Did she dare? Could they? Would he hate her?

She wasn't going to worry about him. She had to look out for herself and the baby. The baby first.

But Sherry was right. Blaire knew she couldn't keep running from Justin, couldn't keep avoiding the question that hung over her head like a two-ton green elephant.

She grabbed her coat and purse and marched out of the bedroom and into the living room.

He looked good, she thought, her mind shooting off course and onto a side rail. He didn't look terribly happy, but he looked good.

"I thought you went home last night," she said.

"I thought you stayed at Connie's today."

Blaire took a slow, deep breath and allowed him the point. "Let's go get a cup of coffee or something."

Justin let out the breath he'd been holding. She was going to talk to him. She was probably going to say no, but at least she was talking.

They took his rig and drove to a nearby coffee

shop. Having skipped breakfast, Justin was starving. He ordered bacon, eggs, hash browns and a short stack of pancakes smothered in butter and syrup.

It was a lot of food for someone as trim and lean as Justin, but Blaire didn't question it. She knew he worked hard on his ranch. Working men needed fuel.

She ordered decaf and a Danish.

"I'm not going to marry you," she said baldly.

Justin felt a wave of disappointment wash through him. "I guess I knew that was coming."

"I'd like to tell you why."

"I'd like to hear it."

Blaire paused a moment to get her thoughts in order. Her cousins knew the story almost as well as she did. Some of them had even lived it in their own homes. But Blaire had never tried to explain it to any-one before. She supposed the best way to start was simply to start.

"My parents had to get married."

"Because she was pregnant with you?"

"That's right. They knew each other better than you and I do, but like us, they'd never talked about getting married. Never really considered it. Then, suddenly, there they were, expectant parents. It's been a disaster ever since."

"What disaster?" Justin said. "They're still mar-ried, aren't they?"

"And the good Lord is the only one who knows why," she said with feeling. "There's not a week that has gone by during my entire life that one or the other or both of them hasn't thrown it up into the other's face. If you hadn't got pregnant…if you hadn't knocked me up…every problem that comes up, health, financial, business, you name it, it's because one of them caused them to have to get married. Now and then they get tired of blaming each other and they turn around and, oh, look, she's the one. It's her fault. If it hadn't been for her we wouldn't have had to get married and we wouldn't be having these problems."

Justin stared, sickened by what she was saying. "They blame you for their own troubles?"

"Constantly. When they're not blaming each other."

"That's awful."

"You're damn right it is," she said hotly. Then she paused and sipped her coffee to give herself time to calm down. "I've seen the same thing happen with two of my cousins whose parents had to get married. I won't ever do that to myself, Justin, or to a child of mine. So you see why I can't marry you."

"You think that would happen to us? That we'd end up resenting each other, taking it out on the kid?"

"I think it's highly likely."

He shook his head. "I don't see it that way."

"That's because you haven't had to live with it the way I have my whole life."

"But you're not your mother, and I'm not your father. And now that we're both aware of what could go wrong, we can take steps to avoid it. We could make it work."

"You don't know that."

"You don't know that we can't."

"I know that for me to marry a man I'm not in love with—no offense—who's not in love with me, is just asking for trouble. Are you in love with me?" she demanded.

"I can't say that I am. Right now. Who's to say I won't be in a few months?"

"You think, what, that my fried chicken will win your heart?"

"You cook? I guess I should have asked that before I suggested we get married."

"Very funny, Chisholm. But don't you see that I'm right? There has to be something other than a baby who's not even born yet to bring us together, to keep us together. Expecting a child to keep us together, that's not fair to the child. No baby should have to shoulder that kind of responsibility."

"I agree." He grinned. "There's hot sex. That'd work for about the next fifty or sixty years."

"Ha. How about the next three or four months. Until I start looking like a beached whale. See how much you want me then."

"Look, Blaire, I understand why you're reluctant to marry me."

"Do you? Look at it this way. Asking me to ignore what my parents have done and marry you anyway just because you tell me to, would be like asking you to forget how your father died and drive home drunk, just because I told you to."

"It's not exactly the same," he said tightly.

Blaire could have kicked herself for bringing up his father's death. What was the matter with her? "I'm sorry. I shouldn't have said that. I think pregnancy puts holes in my brain."

"That's one of my points," he said. "Pregnancy is going to cause a lot of changes for you. You're going to need some help. A little moral support, somebody to rub your back, your feet. Somebody to pay the bills you wouldn't ordinarily have. I can do those things for you. I want to do those things for you."

"Oh, yeah, after you've been up since dawn, out working the cattle, planting hay, and all the other things you do 'til sundown every day. You'll come in beat and hungry. You'll be the one wanting your back rubbed."

He nodded as if in agreement. "And when you're through rubbing mine, and I've had my dinner and a couple of beers and watched the fights on ESPN, if you're still awake I'll rub your back."

"I didn't know you were such a comedian," she said.

"Why don't we do this," he suggested. "You've said no to my proposal. I'll accept that, for now. But I reserve the right to try to change your mind, and to ask again. Agreed?"

"Do I have a choice?"

"Not from where I'm sitting. I like your cousins, by the way. The two I've met so far."

"I'm glad. You'll want to go to Connie's funeral. I'm going to kill her for telling you where I went."

"See? I'm not the only comedian around here."

Justin drove Blaire back to Sherry's apartment. They didn't speak, but the silence was a little easier between them than their conversations had been lately.

Justin was preoccupied with what to do next. He knew, if given enough time, that he could change her mind about marrying him. He desperately wanted this settled between them before he went home. He had to tell his family what was going on before they heard it in town.

Damn. The feed store. Why hadn't he thought of that? If Sloan or Caleb or Grandmother or anybody from the Rose or the Pruitt Ranch went in to the feed store, Blaire's father was likely to jump down their throat, while her mother could very well hug them and welcome them to the family.

He needed to convince Blaire to marry him so they could stop keeping secrets.

"I'm going to ask you again," he told her as he pulled up in her cousin's parking lot.

"Justin, I'm not going to marry you."

"You might change your mind by this time tomorrow. I'll call you."

"You're welcome to call, but I won't change my mind."

"Maybe I'll just call to see how you're feeling. You are feeling all right, aren't you?"

"I'm feeling fine. I'll be feeling fine this time tomorrow, too. You're not one of those guys who has to know where a woman is every hour of the day and what she's doing, are you?"

"No. I'll just want to know you're okay, and if you've changed your mind about marrying me."

"I can save you the trouble. I'll be fine, and I'll be single."

"You're going to be stubborn, aren't you?" he asked.

"In a matter of months I'll be giving up my independence and privacy for the next eighteen to twenty-one years of my life. For the next five or six, at least, I won't even be able to go to the bathroom alone. I don't plan to answer to anyone until then if I can help it."

Justin quirked his lips. "I can't say I blame you. I'll see you in a few days."

"Justin?" she said after he had helped her out of the pickup and was returning to the driver's side.

"Yes?"

"Thank you for asking me to marry you. Even though I said no, and I'll say no again, yours is still my first proposal."

It occurred to Justin as he drove out of the parking lot, keeping his eyes open for a gas station before he decided if he was going home that day or not,

that her second and third proposals were also likely
to be his. In fact, the idea of anyone but him proposing to her didn't sit well with him at all.

Ponca City was an oil refinery town. Finding a gas
station was no problem. He picked one a block before the interstate and pulled up to the pump.

When he got out to fill his tank, the air felt definitely chillier than it had only moments before. He
glanced up at the sky and was surprised that he hadn't
noticed before how dark and gray it had become.

The first snowflakes melted against his face before his tank was full, but as he drove away, it seemed
the sky had changed its mind and decided to hold off
on the snow.

The rest of the day did not turn out at all the way
Justin thought it might. He'd thought he would either
laze around a motel room if Sloan didn't need him
at home, or drive back to the ranch if he did.

It turned out that Sloan did need him, but not at
home.

"Where are you this time?" Sloan asked, aggra-
vation clear in his voice.

"Ponca City."

"Still not going to tell me why?"

"It's personal."

"A woman? You're running all over the damn
state, letting your work pile up by the hour, because
of a woman? Kid, you must have it bad."

"I'll tell you about it when I get home."

"And when might that be?"

"If you need me, I'll come home right now," Justin offered.

"Naw," Sloan admitted. "We're fine. Did you say you were in Ponca City?"

"That's right."

"Maybe you could do us a favor and run over to the Ledbetter Ranch up by Blackwell. You remember the place, don't you?"

"Sure. What's there?"

"They've got a young Hereford bull they've been bragging about, but they're asking a pretty penny for him. Maybe you could take a look at him, check out his pedigree, see if you think he's worth it."

"Sure, I can do that."

"I'll call and set it up."

Sloan made the arrangements and Justin drove up to the Ledbetter Ranch near Blackwell. The bull was good, but not good enough to justify the price, in his opinion.

By the time he finished there it was the middle of the afternoon. He could still drive home, get there just after dark. Or he could stay in Ponca City and go see Blaire the next day rather than merely call her.

He winced at the idea. No, he wouldn't go to Sherry's apartment looking for Blaire. He would call, as

he'd said he would. He would give her that much
space, at least.

He ate a lonely dinner and spent a boring night
watching cable TV in his motel room.

Was he crazy, chasing all over the state after a
woman who didn't want him around?

But was that true? Did she really not want him
around, or was she only afraid to take a gamble on him?

And why shouldn't she be leery of such a thing?
What had he ever done to earn her trust?

Around and around in circles his mind went until
he came up with the conclusion that he had no business following her around from cousin to cousin this
way. It made him feel like a jerk. A desperate jerk,
at that.

Blaire tossed and turned half the night, wondering if she was doing the right thing. Maybe she
should be practical and say yes to Justin.

No. No. She refused to allow herself to end up like
her mother, turn Justin into a bitter man like her father. Make their child feel as if he or she is to blame
for everything that goes wrong.

That way lay disaster.

Perhaps her mother wouldn't have made it on her
own. Maybe she'd had no real choice but to marry.

But Blaire was not her mother. She had a college
degree, a teaching certificate and good references.
Once the baby was born she would surely be able to

find a new teaching position. If not, she was more than capable of doing other work.

She didn't need to be married to survive. She was a firm believer that marriage solely for the sake of the children was one of society's most horrendous mistakes.

But it was hard, turning away a man she'd been attracted to since she'd been in high school.

Remembering their conversation at the Mexican restaurant the other night, she smiled. He had wondered why they hadn't met years ago. That they hadn't had been Blaire's doing. He didn't remember her, but she would never forget him.

She'd been so shy back then, the new girl in a small school, when her dad had bought the feed store and moved them to Rose Rock. Justin had been out of school by the time she came to town, but she saw him anyway. He came to high school football games, rode in the county rodeos, played on local softball teams, bought feed and supplies at her father's feed store. She'd seen him everywhere. She had followed him with her eyes, and her young heart.

She hadn't had the nerve to introduce herself or do anything to draw his attention.

He hadn't wanted for female attention, however. There'd been a different girl on his arm every other time he showed up in town. In between each new girl, there was always Melanie.

Melanie Pruitt of the Pruitt Ranch. It was public

knowledge back then that Melanie had her sights set on the eldest Chisholm, Sloan. But while the girl waited for Sloan to come to his senses and fall in love with her, she told her troubles to Caleb, and ran around with Justin. Melanie and Justin were a twosome as often as not.

If anyone had asked Blaire, she would have said Melanie was out of her mind to pine after Sloan when Justin was there and available. Not that there was anything wrong with Sloan, but Justin…well, be still, her heart.

By the time Blaire finished high school she'd conquered her shyness, and set her puppy love for Justin Chisholm aside. That man wasn't about to go anywhere without his best friend Melanie.

It seemed to Blaire there might be a lot more going on between those two than mere friendship.

Blaire had gone with other boys, moved away to college, found a good job in Oklahoma City, had a full life.

Then her mother had broken her arm and Blaire had come home. She would never forget that first day back in town, standing in the middle of the feed store office, where her mother normally ruled, staring in shock at the mess her father had made in the few days her mother had been out.

She'd heard the bell over the store's front door jingle, announcing a customer. She needn't worry; her father was out there to take care of business.

Then she'd heard that voice, so deep and smooth and clear. She hadn't realized she had been carrying his voice around inside her all those years, but there it was. Justin Chisholm was in the store.

She had sworn to herself that she was *not* going to peek around the door frame. She would have been entirely too mortified to live if he caught her.

It hadn't been too many weeks, however, before she realized he was eyeing her, checking her out. She'd been astounded. Delighted. And suddenly shy again, the insecure new kid.

It wasn't lost on her that he and Melanie were, as always, the closest of…companions.

That being the case, Blaire hadn't for a moment thought he meant to pay her any serious attention, so she had swallowed her shyness and played it cool. If every girl in town fell at his feet—and they did—and if he had Melanie for backup—Blaire would play hard to get.

Not that she thought for a minute that it would get her anywhere with him, but it might keep her from ending up with a broken heart.

She'd been wrong. About several things.

Melanie, it seemed, was never in love with Justin, nor he with her. She'd given up on Sloan some time in the past, and early in December had up and married Caleb, the middle Chisholm brother.

Justin did not seem in the least heartbroken. In fact, he seemed pleased.

Since that was the case, Blaire had decided to stop playing so hard to get. She let herself be caught.

Now she carried his child, and he wanted to marry her for all the wrong reasons. She was bound to end up with a broken heart, one way or another, before they settled things between them.

He'd said he would call her tomorrow. If he ran true to form, he wouldn't call, he would show up at the door. If she ran true to form, she wouldn't be there.

Chapter Seven

Eventually they both ran true to form.

Blaire left Sherry's apartment before it was light, headed to Stillwater, just over forty miles south down the two-lane blacktop, to her cousin Gayle's. The grass was covered with snow, and the white stuff was starting to stick to the pavement.

But she had only forty miles to go. No problem.

She pulled out of Sherry's parking lot and went on her merry way. Sneaking out, again, like a thief in the night, running away from a man she thought more and more might be the one she should hold on to.

Justin saw the snow when he got up. He shrugged. Not enough to worry about, especially since he would be taking the interstate most of the way home.

It was too early to call Blaire, so he walked across the street to the restaurant for breakfast. Afterward he went back to his room to check in with Sloan, noticing on the way that the snow was getting heavier.

At home Sloan said that the snow was heavy and piling up fast.

Justin swore at himself. He should have gone home last night, damn his hide. He would call Blaire, as he'd promised, then head back.

Simple plan.

Not so simple in application.

Blaire was gone.

Dammit, why hadn't he seen it coming?

"Did she say where she was going?" he asked Cousin Sherry.

"The note she left said she was going to stop in on Gayle before heading home. Is something wrong?"

He glanced out the window of his motel room at the snow that was starting to swirl in the increasing wind.

"Have you looked outside lately?" he asked tersely.

There was a rustling sound, then the slight *clink* made when someone shifted a few slats of window blinds up or down. "Oh, my," she said. "There must be two inches already, except the wind's blowing it sideways, so it's hard to tell. Wow."

"Sherry," he snapped. He had the feeling if he didn't stop her, she'd go on and on about the snow for another ten minutes. "Blaire? What time did she leave?"

"Oh. Blaire. I don't know, really. We were going to sleep late, so that's what I did. I woke up just a few minutes ago. She could have been gone an hour, or three. But she was only going to Stillwater. I'm sure she got there before things got this nasty."

"Will you do me a favor and call this other cousin and see if Blaire made it? Or give me the number and I'll call."

"Oh, I'll call. I can tell you're worried, so I'm getting worried, too. Call me back in five."

The line went dead in Justin's ear.

Four minutes later he redialed Sherry's number.

"What did they say?" he demanded.

"Okay," Sherry said. "Now I'm worried. She isn't there yet. In fact, nobody's there. There was no answer, and Blaire hasn't called or anything."

"Wouldn't she have called Gayle before going down there?"

"No. Not calling, that's no big deal. We show up on each other's doorsteps all the time in this family. But it's less than an hour's drive from here to Gayle's. Maybe Blaire stopped to eat on the way. I'm sure she's fine."

"Does she have a cell phone with her?" He could

have kicked himself for not making that his first question ten minutes ago.

"Blaire's one of those Neanderthal throwbacks, meaning she doesn't have a cell phone. How anyone can function in this day and age—"

"Sherry." The girl was nice enough, but she had the attention span of a gnat. "Tell me how to get to Gayle's. The way Blaire would go."

He got the directions and address from Sherry and said he would let her know when he found Blaire.

"Do you think she's all right?" Sherry asked, concern plain in her voice.

"I'm sure she's fine," he said, not sure at all. "She's a smart lady. She can take care of herself."

"That's right," Sherry said. "She's real good at that. But still, I'll feel better when I hear from her, or you. You promise you'll call?"

"I promise. As soon as I find her."

Justin wasn't worried about negotiating the snowy roads in his pickup. His tires were new, and he carried an extra four hundred pounds of sandbags in the bed all winter just for such occasions. That weighed him down enough that he didn't slip and slide as much as a pickup with an empty bed.

But he didn't have as much confidence in Blaire's little red compact. That thing was a tin can on wheels, and he had no idea how much tread she had on her tires. Hell, a good gust of wind, and there were plenty of those today, could blow her off the road.

He drove the distance between Ponca City and Stillwater via U.S. Highway 177, the route Sherry said Blaire would take. There was considerably more traffic than there should have been, considering the weather, and it was creeping along at a snail's pace. Except for the idiots who passed them going eighty on snow-slicked roads, sending up a rooster tail of snow and slush flinging across each windshield they passed, effectively blinding every driver for long, long seconds.

Justin thought longingly about the shotgun he'd left at home. He was sure the other drivers on the road would vouch for him that it was justifiable homicide.

He passed three vehicles off in the bar ditch, but they all looked abandoned, and none was a little red two-door with the mother of his unborn child huddling inside.

All in all it took him an hour and a half to drive the forty miles from cousin number two to cousin number three. If anyone asked his opinion, he would have to say that the north central part of Oklahoma was being hit now by a full-fledged blizzard. The snow was razor sharp and blowing sideways.

Judging by the condition of the snow on the ground, Justin was the first person to drive on Cousin Gayle's street in some time.

He told himself that if Blaire had left early enough this morning, she could easily have gotten here before the storm worsened.

He pulled up at the house whose number matched the one Sherry gave him and felt his hopes fade. No little red car sat in the driveway.

When you visited a cousin, did you park in her garage? None of his cousins would have let him take their protected space. In any case, there were no telltale depressions in the snow of the driveway to indicate anyone had driven on it at all.

He got out and made his way to the front door, where he rang the doorbell, then pounded and pounded and got no answer.

Back in his truck, he unclipped his cell phone from his belt and called Sherry.

"Nobody's home," he said tersely. "Have you heard from her?"

"No," Sherry said. "I haven't heard from anybody. You say nobody's home?"

"No one answers the door."

"That's odd. Is there a green SUV in the driveway?"

"Nothing in the driveway but smooth snow. Nobody's driven on it in a while."

"Then Gayle's not there, and if she's not there, nobody's there."

"Where would Blaire go if she got here and found Gayle gone?"

"She'd either come back here, or go back to Connie's, but that's not likely. She might just go home. She said she was going home tomorrow anyway."

Fear was not something Justin felt often, but now it was here and it was huge. Blaire was out there driving around in this damn blizzard in a tin can on wheels, with no cell phone to call for help if she needed it.

"What are you going to do?" Sherry asked.

"I'm going to find her."

But which way to go? he wondered after disconnecting the call. Back north toward Ponca City, or west toward the interstate? Surely if she headed home it would be via the interstate. It had to have been snowing by the time she made it to Gayle's. She wouldn't have stuck to the back roads and two-lane highways in this weather.

Would she?

No. He'd told Sherry that Blaire was smart, and she was. He had to assume that she would use her head.

But since she had left Sherry's this morning instead of waiting for the call she knew he would make, then she was running partly on emotion.

Had she been afraid he would show up, as he had at Connie's and Sherry's? If that's what she thought, and she hadn't wanted to talk to him anymore for the time being, then she would have left without a qualm. Or with only a few qualms, at the most.

After driving to Stillwater, with bad weather starting, she would have no reason to go back to Ponca City, where she'd known him to be.

No, he thought, starting his engine and driving out of the quiet, snow covered neighborhood. Blaire was headed home.

Justin intended to follow.

Blaire gripped the steering wheel so hard her knuckles threatened to break through her thin leather gloves. The blinding snow was bad enough without having a car or truck whiz past her in the left lane and stir it all up even worse.

The road was a solid sheet of ice. Driving conditions hadn't been this bad just five miles back down the road when she'd left Stillwater and headed west for the interstate. It had apparently been snowing out here longer. Already there were snow drifts along the shoulders.

She was getting worried about what kind of shape I-35 would be in when she finally reached it. She had only another ten or fifteen miles to go, but it was going to take her forever. Her car was not designed for driving fast under these conditions.

She was an idiot and a coward. She should have stayed at Sherry's and let Justin call or show up, whichever he planned. But no, she'd had to run. Again.

Not wanting to wake Gayle if she'd worked late last night, Blaire had stopped on the outskirts of Stillwater and called. She'd gotten no answer.

She didn't know where Gayle was, but Blaire had decided it was just as well that she wasn't there. It was time to go home. The snow wasn't bad.

She would have checked the weather on her radio, but her radio hadn't worked in months. A bad mistake, not getting it fixed. She knew that now. Knowing that they were in for a genuine blizzard, she would not have left Stillwater, unless it had been to go back north to Ponca City and Sherry's.

But she hadn't known, had misjudged, and now had to fight to keep her car on the road.

She saw in her rearview mirror the tractor-trailer rig racing up behind her as if she were sitting still. Alarmed, she started easing toward the shoulder.

At the last instant the semi swerved into the left lane to avoid hitting her.

It missed hitting her, thank God, but the gust of wind in its wake was enough, when coupled with the slick road and the fact that the tires on the right side of Blaire's car were on the shoulder instead of the highway, to send her off the road completely.

Blaire cried out and fought the need to slam on the brakes, which would only make her skid and lose control altogether.

As if she had any control to lose, she thought with growing panic. The left tires, still on the pavement, had nothing to grip but ice and snow. Her right tires sank in the snow to the muddy grass beneath and pulled her completely off the road and down the slope, sliding nose-first toward a snow-filled ditch.

She tried to steer away. She tried tapping the brakes to slow her decent. Nothing helped. In desperation she jerked the steering wheel. The action slammed her passenger door against a tree. She jerked the wheel in the opposite direction, knowing even as she did that she shouldn't.

The car swerved on the slope, turned completely backward until she was facing back toward Stillwater, but sliding sideways down the slope.

She came to a crashing halt with her driver's door slammed against the far side of the ditch, her car tilting at a forty-five-degree angle, driver's side down.

Justin drove the main streets through Stillwater on his way to the highway that would take him to the interstate and home. He kept an eye out for Blaire, but didn't see her. Seeing farther ahead than twenty yards was getting more difficult by the minute.

Other than a few semis, there was little traffic on the highway heading west out of town, but lack of visibility made the going slow. Justin drove slower than necessary so he could keep a close eye out for any little red car that might have slid off the icy-slick pavement.

He nearly slid off himself a time or two. He couldn't imagine driving in these conditions in that toy she called a car.

The highway here was four-lane divided. He stayed in the righthand lane, but tried to watch the median, too, in case she'd gone off there.

Of course she might not have had any trouble at all. She might be halfway home by now, or holed up in some snug motel along the interstate, or even at one behind him in Stillwater, although he doubted the latter.

A tractor-trailer rig barreled past on Justin's left, blinding him for long seconds in the backwash of snow kicked up by all eighteen wheels and thrown directly onto Justin's windshield.

He almost missed it. Just before the world outside his truck turned completely white, he thought he caught a glimpse of a red fender sticking up out of the ditch at the bottom of a slope off the right shoulder.

Justin gripped the steering wheel and eased off the highway and to a stop on the shoulder. When the solid cloud of snow generated by the passing semi cleared, leaving only the blizzard—enough of a visibility reducer on its own—he was about fifty yards beyond where he thought he'd seen the red car, but he couldn't be sure because he couldn't see fifty yards. He couldn't see twenty.

He backed up a few yards, then had to stop when he spotted a cut in the shoulder where a culvert ran beneath the highway for drainage.

He parked, killed the engine, and after bundling up, hiked back to see if he'd been imagining things.

He hadn't been imagining things. There was, indeed, a little red car stuck driver's side down in the ditch at the bottom of the steep slope.

Justin's heart took a leap and lodged halfway up his throat.

* * *

Blaire sat huddled inside her car trying to think positive thoughts. Surely someone would see her car before it became completely buried in snow. Surely.

But what were the chances?

Still, she had hope.

As near as she could guess, she'd been stuck where she was for less than thirty minutes. Cold was seeping into the car, but it wasn't deadly. Yet. She would start the engine in a few minutes. She was a little hesitant about that, because she didn't know if her tailpipe was clogged with snow or not. If it was, deadly carbon monoxide fumes would fill the car and she would never know it. She would just get sleepy, then die.

She would have gotten out and flagged down help, but she couldn't get out. Her car lay at a forty-five-degree angle, with the weight of it resting on the driver's side, her door pressed into the bank of the ditch.

The car was small enough that she could get to the passenger door, but her earlier encounter with the tree rendered the door useless. It was good and dented and stuck. The window wouldn't roll down, the door wouldn't open.

If no one came to her aid soon, she would have to try to kick out the windshield, or the back window, or the passenger window. She wondered if she could even do it. Sneakers weren't the preferred shoe for such a stunt.

Still, she would try, because she had no intension of sitting here and freezing to death.

She wondered where Justin was. Nowhere near here, that was for sure. He was either up at Ponca City or halfway back to the Cherokee Rose by now. And he was probably ticked at her for running out on him again.

She was none too pleased with herself for doing it, but it was a done deal now. And look where it had gotten her.

If the damn forecasters had given a little warning on last night's newscast, she might have been a little more prepared to survive the day. As it was, she had a medium weight coat, thin leather gloves, and that was it. Her feet, in her sneakers, were going to freeze when she got out. If she got out.

No. Not if. When.

So be it. Her only other option was to sit and wait for the spring thaw.

She was saying a brief but sincere prayer for the well-being of her baby, when suddenly a large chunk of snow covering her windshield disappeared. A face loomed there.

Blaire screamed.

The face jerked away. "Blaire!"

Justin? That couldn't have been Justin's voice.

"Blaire!" His face reappeared. It *was* Justin!

"Justin?"

"Blaire! Are you all right?"

"I'm fine, I'm fine," she assured. "I'm just trapped in here. I can't get out."

"Are you hurt?"

"No. No, I'm fine. What are you doing here?"

"I'm looking for you. What happened? Were you hit? Are you hurt?"

His obvious concern warmed her heart. Some of that had to be for her, Blaire, not just for the mother of his unborn child.

"I'm not hurt," she assured him. "I was driving along just fine, slow, but fine, when some joker in a semi whizzed by and rocked my poor little car like it was a toy."

"Well?"

"Hey, don't you make fun of my car."

"You can finish your story later," he said. "Gather what you need and let's get you out of there."

"How? The passenger door is jammed."

"Are you sure?" He gave the door a tug and nothing happened.

"I couldn't get it open," she told him.

"Hang on." He tried it again, and still, nothing happened. "All right," he said to the door. He braced his foot on the frame beside the door and pulled with all his might.

The door popped open.

Justin went sprawling, disappearing from Blaire's view.

"Justin!" she cried. She scrambled up the slope of

the passenger seat until she could see out the newly opened door. "Justin?"

"I'm here." Disgusted, he pushed himself to his feet and brushed snow from his hair, his coat, his jeans. Dug it out of his ear.

"Are you all right?"

"I'm fine," he snarled. He had snow down his back. He hated getting snow down his back. And it was easier to deal with being angry about falling down than the fear he'd tasted when he had spotted her car down here in this ditch.

"Pass your bags or whatever out to me," he called.

He heard a grunt, then a curse, then a midsize duffel bag appeared in the open door, followed shortly by a smaller overnight case, then by Blaire herself.

For the first time since spotting her car, he was able to take an easy breath. He could now see for himself that she was all right.

"Hold on." He propped the duffel and overnighter on the front fender, then reached for her. "Let me help you." He grasped her beneath her arms and lifted her out of the car. It took all his strength to stand her beside him on the snowy slope and release her, when what he wanted to do was hold her close and make sure she stayed safe.

But he did find the strength, he did release her. He grabbed her bag and case and motioned for her to start up the slope ahead of him. "It's slick, so take it slow."

She took it slow, but that didn't stop her from sliding back down into his legs. He went down, and the two of them ended up in a pile against her car.

When the grunting, groaning, and swearing was over with, they took stock.

"Are you hurt?" he demanded, helping her stand.

"No." She shook snow from her head. "You?"

"I'm fine." But he wondered how many times a pregnant woman could be bounced around—hit a tree, slide into a ditch, tumble down a slope—and still be truly fine. "Are you sure you're all right?"

"I'm sure." She put the strap of her shoulder bag over her head and turned to face the slope. "Ten bucks says I make it this time."

"No bet. Let's just get up to the road and into the pickup before my nose freezes off."

Through the blowing snow she tossed him a grin over her shoulder. "Wimp."

Justin started up after her, telling himself that if she could grin at him under the current circumstances, she couldn't be hurt too badly. In fact, she didn't appear to be hurt at all. It was only his own worry that nagged at him.

They made it to the top of the slope and the shoulder of the highway this time, Blaire more easily because she could use her hands to help her climb up, while Justin was hampered by her duffel and overnight case. Still, he was only a couple of minutes behind her.

"Justin?" She turned toward him and squinted against the blowing snow. She had to shout to be heard over the howling of the wind now that they were up and out of the relative protection of the ditch. "Where's your pickup?"

"Up there." Justin nodded toward where he had parked, then realized that visibility was even worse now than it had been a few minutes ago. He couldn't see his pickup at all. "I think."

He slogged his way up the shoulder through the ever deepening snow, over the culvert, and there, abruptly, sat his rig. He let out the breath he hadn't realized he'd been holding.

"Here we are," he shouted. He led Blaire to the passenger door and helped her up into the cab. He tucked her bag and case around her feet, then circled the truck and climbed in. He started the engine and cranked the heat up to high.

"I vote we go back to Stillwater and get a room until this blows over." Justin glanced over at Blaire to measure her reaction.

She sat huddled in on herself, her feet stretched out toward the hot air blasting from his heater.

"Blaire?"

"As long as it's warm and comes with something hot to drink, and I'm trying to stay away from caffeine because of the baby."

"A warm room, and something hot to drink. You got it. Anything else?"

"Not that I can think of. And Justin?"

"Yeah?"

"I don't know how you found me or what you were doing on this highway, but thank you."

"You're welcome," he told her. "I was looking for you."

"I'm sorry."

"For what?" he asked, surprised by the apology.

"For causing all this trouble. Can I ask you a question?"

"You can ask me anything. We're trying to get to know each other better, aren't we?"

"I suppose."

"What did you want to ask?"

"This morning. You were going to call me again?"

"Yes."

"Did you? Call I mean. Or did you go to the apartment?"

He smiled slightly. "I decided it was time to act like a grown-up and call, the way I said I would. So that's what I did."

"Oh." Her face fell. "While I ran off, acting childish again."

"That's not what I said. And it's not what I meant," he assured her. "Anyway, acting like a grown-up nearly killed me."

She smiled slightly. "That's comforting."

Justin pulled in at the first decent motel they came to. The parking lot was filled with snow-covered cars. The chances of a vacancy looked slim, but Justin went into the office anyway to check.

Blaire stayed in the pickup, trying her best to soak up the heat from the heater. She could barely see Justin through the layer of ice covering the motel window. He was filling out a form or card or something, so he must have gotten them a room.

Blaire was relieved. She was no sissy when it came to driving in bad weather, but this was simply too dangerous. Plus, the stress of her accident had somehow sapped all her energy. She felt as limp as a noodle. And cold clear down to the marrow in her bones.

Inside the motel office, Justin was told that because of the storm, he was getting the last available motel room in town.

He doubted it was the very last one in town, but it appeared to be the last one in this motel, and he wasn't inclined to drive from motel to motel to look for one with two vacant rooms.

Blaire hadn't said she expected a separate room and he hadn't offered one. But it would have been nice if she'd had a choice. Now she would have none. She would have to share with him.

Maybe, if he behaved himself, they could use the time together to get to know each other better.

"I'm sorry," he told her when he got back into the pickup. "I tried to get two rooms. I thought you might prefer your privacy. But they're full up because of the storm. They had one room left."

"It's all right, Justin. We'll manage."

For her part, Blaire was not surprised to find herself sharing a motel room with Justin again. A little nervous. Okay, maybe a lot nervous. But under the circumstances, it seemed inevitable. He had trailed her all over the state, and now they were stuck in a blizzard nearly two hundred miles from home.

There was a deeper concern at work in the back of her mind: Had she fled to Enid hoping he would follow?

Ridiculous. She'd had no reason to think he would come after her. Why should he do such a thing?

Why *did* he do such a thing?

She sat next to him as he followed the manager's directions to their room and parked near the end of the building.

Blaire gathered her duffel bag and overnight case in her arms and prepared to get out.

"I'll get those," Justin said tersely.

She had accepted more help from him lately than she had ever accepted from another soul. It made her uncomfortable. "Thanks," she said, "but I've already got them." She opened the passenger door and climbed down before Justin could stop her.

He joined her on the sidewalk with his own belongings carried in two blue Wal-Mart shopping bags.

"Nice luggage," she teased.

"Like it?" He tucked one bag under his arm and unlocked the door to their room. "After you."

Blaire stepped into the room and placed her luggage on the only bed, a king.

Justin followed her and plopped his two sacks on the dresser. "When I left home I thought I was only going to town. I had to do some shopping in Enid. I didn't even have a toothbrush with me. Now I have everything I need." He patted the blue plastic. "Are you warm yet?" he asked her.

"Yes. Thank you. The heater in your pickup is great."

"Then I guess the next thing we need to see to is feeding you. I assume you're hungry."

"Starving."

"There's a restaurant right next door. You may think I'm crazy, but I think we should drive. It's far enough over there to freeze your nose off on the way."

"I vote we drive," she said.

"It's unanimous then. Just let me call home first and let them know where I am." He reached for his cell phone. "Do you want to call your parents?"

"No, thanks." She shook her head. "I don't think my father would appreciate hearing I'm sharing a motel room with you."

"Well, I would hope you wouldn't put it quite that way."

"They think I'm with one of my cousins. I'll just let them think that for a while longer," she said.

He made his call, then called Sherry, then they went back out into the storm and climbed into the pickup. Blaire was grateful for the ride, as the snow was even heavier, the temperature lower than it had been only a few minutes earlier.

Over a meal of pot roast, mashed potatoes and gravy for her and beef stew and corn bread for him, Justin entertained Blaire with stories of growing up on the Cherokee Rose the youngest of three brothers.

An excellent swimmer herself, Blaire winced at the story of how Sloan and Caleb had taught Justin to swim at the age of three by throwing him head-first into the stock pond.

"You could have been killed. Drowned, broken neck, water moccasin, anything," she cried in protest.

"Naw," he said. "We were in the middle of a five-year drought. The water was only about two feet deep. I could have suffocated in the mud and the muck, but they dragged me out."

Blaire shuddered. "Remind me not to let our child around its uncles until after he or she learns to swim."

"Not to worry," Justin told her. "When Grandmother found out what they'd done she made them go down by the creek and cut their own willow switches and gave them a licking they still talk about in whispers. Besides, they're older and wiser now. Well, older, anyway."

Blaire chuckled as she knew she was meant to. Then she wondered aloud. "Do they know about the baby? Your brothers, I mean. The rest of your family."

"No." He shook his head. "They know some-thing's going on, but not what."

Blaire frowned. "What do they think's going on? What have you told them?"

"I haven't told them anything. They're just observant, that's all. They know that for the past couple of months, when you wouldn't take or return my calls, much less go out with me again, I've been miserable."

Blaire started, blinked. "Really?"

He shrugged. "My brothers read me pretty well, but there's no hiding anything from Emily. That woman knows everything. She's amazing. Scary, even."

Blaire hadn't been questioning his family's ability to determine his moods, she'd been astounded to hear him state so matter-of-factly that he'd been miserable—because of her.

Wow. That merited some serious consideration. Did he perhaps care for her, a little? During those two months he said he'd been miserable, he hadn't known about the baby. If he had indeed been miserable, it could only have been because of her. Couldn't it?

Unless he was stringing her along. Men did that to women all the time.

Oh, she could drive herself crazy trying to read his mind. Or know his heart.

"What's wrong?" he asked.

She shook her head. "Nothing. Sorry. My mind wandered."

"I must not be much of a conversationalist."

"It's not that," she said quickly. "I'm just tired. I

didn't get much sleep last night, and today's been a little on the stressful side."

"When we get back to the room you should take a nap."

"Thanks." She gave him a wry smile. "But that won't work."

"Why not?"

"I can only sleep if it's quiet and dark. Unless you want to sit in the dark without making any noise, I won't get any sleep until tonight. Don't worry about it. Maybe we can find a good movie on TV to pass the time."

"I've probably got a deck of cards in the glove box of my rig."

"That might come in handy."

"We'll figure it out," he told her. "Besides. After this meal, I may want a nap myself. You're not the only one who hasn't had much sleep lately."

The look he gave her told her she was the reason for his recent lack of sleep.

Was he serious? Did he mean it?

Why couldn't she just take a man—this man, at least—at his word, take his words at face value? Why did she have to question everything, doubt him and her-self, fear lies and deception where none were intended?

"How about dessert?" Justin suggested.

If it would delay the time when she would have to be alone with him… "Yes. Please. That sounds great."

Not that she didn't want to be alone with him. That

was the problem. She did want to. But she was so afraid of making a fool of herself that she feared to even try.

"You're zoning out again," he said.

"Sorry." She shook her head. "I guess I'm more tired than I thought."

"Are you sure it's not something else?"

The look in his eyes said if she gave him half a chance he could read her mind like an open book.

"Something else like what?"

"Like maybe you're not feeling well?"

"No, I'm fine, honest."

He let it go, and the waitress came and took their dessert order. A few minutes later the woman delivered Justin's carrot cake and Blaire's peach cobbler.

"How do you feel," Justin asked, "about my spending a little money on you?"

Blaire frowned. "You want to buy me something?"

"I want to get you a cell phone. If you'd had one today you wouldn't have had to wait for someone to come along and help you."

"You want," she said slowly, "to get me a cell phone?" The idea was too logical to argue with. She needed one. But she wasn't prepared to start accepting gifts from him. She scrambled around in her head trying to figure out a way to afford not only the phone but the monthly service.

"And the monthly service that goes with it," he added, as if, indeed, reading her mind.

Letting him buy her a phone was one thing, she

thought, but allowing him to pay for the monthly service, too? That would give him a hold over her that she wasn't quite comfortable with.

"You're right that I need the phone," she told him. "I'll check into getting one when I get home."

"Meaning you don't want me to take care of it?"

"Meaning I'm not prepared to let you start spending money right and left on me."

"I guess I can understand that," he said. "But if I want to spend money on the baby, you're going to find it impossible to stop me."

She smiled. "The baby's a little young to have his or her own phone, don't you think?"

Justin let out a long breath and shook his head. "Are you going to let me pay for this meal, or did you want to handle that yourself, too?"

She might have taken offense at his remark, or thought that he was serious, but she saw the twinkle in his eyes.

"I don't mind if you buy us a meal. You are indirectly feeding the baby, after all."

"That eating-for-two stuff, is that true?"

"Pretty much. Eating for two, sleeping for two, peeing for two. I can't wait to see what the next seven months bring."

"And after that, things'll get really interesting," Justin predicted. "For about the next thirty years."

Chapter Eight

When they returned to the motel room, Blaire hung up her coat in what passed for a closet area, then sagged on the bed.

"Kick your shoes off and stretch out for a while, why don't you?" Justin suggested. He didn't like the look of those dark circles that were forming beneath her eyes.

She sighed. "I think I'll do just that. What about you?"

"I'm going to join you. I think I feel a nap coming on."

She smiled at him and toed off her sneakers. "You're humoring me so I'll take a nap."

"Am I?" He hung his coat next to hers.

"But it's okay." She let out another sigh and lay down, punching the pillow beneath her head until it was comfortable. "I don't mind. This time."

Justin studied her, tilting his head in thought. "You're not uncomfortable sharing a room with me like this?"

"No." She arched a brow. "Should I be?"

"No, you shouldn't be. But I guess, with the way you've been running off to visit one cousin then another rather than sit down and talk to me, I thought you might be uncomfortable stuck in close quarters with me this way."

"Since you put it that way, I guess maybe I should be. But what can happen? We've already talked, you've asked, I've said no. And I'm already pregnant. What's left to happen?"

He stared at her for a long moment then snapped his gaping mouth shut. "You're kidding, right?"

"Of course not. What do you mean?"

Justin shook his head. "You think because you've said you won't marry me, and because you're already pregnant, that I all of a sudden don't want you anymore?"

Her eyes widened. "You don't…what?"

"I think you heard me."

"I think I did, too, but I'm not sure I understand."

"I'm not sure I do, either. Is that what you think? That you're already pregnant so why bother making love anymore?"

"Oh, boy." She sat up, sat cross-legged on the bed and, groaning, buried her face in her hands. "Does that sound as stupid to you as it does to me?"

Justin sat in the lone chair, which occupied the corner beside the window. "I'm not sure I would use the word stupid, but then, I don't know what word I would use. Alarming, maybe."

She chuckled.

"So maybe you could explain to me what you really meant," he said.

Blaire sat there another minute, breathing in, breathing out. What had she meant, if not the obvious, that she didn't expect him to want her anymore? He wanted to marry her, didn't he? Why would he want to marry her if he didn't want to sleep with her anymore? And sex was the most basic way to bind a man and woman together. At least for a while. So it stood to reason that he would want to sleep with her.

So why *was* she so comfortable sharing a room—a room with one bed—with the man she was highly attracted to? What enormous conceit made her think she could keep him at arm's length if he wanted her?

What idiocy made her even think of keeping him at arm's length in the first place?

"Okay." She raised her head and looked at him. "I take it back. I'm not all that comfortable sharing a room, and a bed, with you."

Justin dropped his head against the wall behind his chair. "That wasn't exactly the outcome I was hoping for."

"Oh, really? Just what were you hoping for? An invitation? Did you expect me to pat the bed?" She patted the bed at a spot right next to her hip. "Come on over here, big boy? Let's have a good time? Is that what you thought would happen?"

He let out a bark of laughter. "No, that is not what I thought would happen. It's not what I expected. It's not even what I hoped for."

She smiled slightly. "How deep do you want to dig this hole you're in?"

He stared up at the ceiling. "I can't win now, no matter what I say."

"True, but I'd like to see how you think you can get yourself out of it."

He took a breath and raised his head to meet her gaze. "I was hoping we could act like two mature adults who happened to be sharing a room through no design of either of them. I was hoping we could try being friends. I was not hoping to get you naked in bed." He held up a hand to stop her from interrupting. "That does not mean I wouldn't very much like to get you naked in bed, because I would. But that isn't why we're here."

"Unlike that night a couple of months ago, right? You got that motel room for the specific purpose of getting me naked and in bed."

"No, but even if I did, where else were we supposed to go for privacy?"

"You had the room booked before you picked me up that night."

"And you think I did that because I planned from the beginning to get you into bed?"

She tilted her head and frowned. "Didn't you?"

His lips quirked. "I'd be lying if I said I hadn't thought about it. I did have hope, but that wasn't why I booked that room. You think I was that sure of myself?"

She shrugged and looked away. "I thought maybe you were that sure of me."

"What?" he cried, rising from the chair. "Sure of you? Woman, I have never been so unsure of anything in my life as I have been of you from the very beginning. Why would I think you were willing to go to bed with me?"

"Because I was? That's exactly where we ended up, isn't it?"

"You think I knew that was going to happen?"

"If you didn't," she said carefully, "how did we end up in a motel room you had already booked?"

"Damn, Blaire, has that been eating at you all these weeks? Everybody in town knows that none of us in my family drives home if we've had more than two beers to drink within two hours of going home. Any more than that and we stay the night in town."

Blaire felt heat sweep up her face. "Because of your father."

"That's right. You didn't know? I thought everybody knew. It's been a topic of conversation around town for years. I can't tell you how many times one or all of us have ended up the butt of some yahoo's stupid joke."

"But you're all live butts."

"Exactly. It's a pact between us, and we never break it."

"A pact? Like, what, a blood oath?"

"A blood oath is just what it is. I imagine Sloan and Caleb had one between the two of them when I was little. But when I turned about twelve, we made a pact among the three of us that we would never end up wrapped around a telephone pole like our dad did when I was a baby, from driving when we'd had too much to drink. We vowed we would never do that to each other. And by damn, we've kept that vow, and we always will."

"And you knew, that night before you picked me up, that you'd be drinking because we were going to hear that rock and roll band, Squatty and the Bodies, at the Road Hog."

"That's right. There's a law or something against listening to sixties rock in a bar and not drinking beer."

"I'm sure there is. I had a few that night myself."

"And we got closer as the night went on," he said, his voice softening, deepening. He moved to stand next to the bed so he could touch her cheek with the tip of one finger.

The touch went all through her, a hot shiver that raised gooseflesh along her arms. She was grateful for her long sleeved sweater, so he could not see what he did to her.

"I remember telling you I had a room," he said, "asking you if you would go there with me."

"Yes." Her mouth and throat dried out. She remembered every second of that night vividly. Her body remembered, too.

"When you said yes," he whispered, "I thought I'd died and gone to heaven."

Her smile may have wobbled, but it was still a smile. "When you asked, I thought the same thing."

He tilted his head back and closed his eyes. "I know I said that I wanted this time, in this room, to be friendly, but if we don't change the subject real quick…"

Realizing how right he was, that they were treading on shaky ground, Blaire swallowed. "As soon as we get home," she said in a rush, "I'll check the prices on cell phones and service plans. If I need help paying for it I'll let you know."

He took a step away from the bed and stuffed his hands into his hip pockets. "Thank you. About the phone, and for the change of subject."

"You're welcome, for both. And thank you, for the warning. I think I'll try that nap now."

"Okay." With a nod, he took another step back. "Will it bother you too much if I read the paper?"

She shook her head. "I probably won't sleep anyway, so don't worry about it. Resting will be enough."

She was still, her breathing even, in fewer than ten minutes, despite the occasional rustle of the newspaper coming from the corner where Justin sat in the stiff, uncomfortable chair.

But Justin, too, was tired. From lack of sleep, lack of physical activity. He wasn't used to sitting around all day, and that's all he'd done for the past couple of days.

Carefully, and as quietly as possible, he folded the newspaper and placed it on the small table next to his chair.

Blaire lay curled on her side on the far side of the bed, her back to him and the rest of the room. If she opened her eyes, she had nothing to see but a blank wall barely two feet from the bed.

Even without being able to see her face, he knew she didn't open her eyes. Her breathing was deep and regular. The stiffness had gone from her shoulders.

He hadn't realized how tight her shoulders had been until he now saw them relaxed.

She was sound asleep.

So much for her not being able to sleep unless it was dark and quiet.

Of course, the only light in the room was the hanging lamp over the table in front of the window, right next to him. And the only sounds had been his rustling of the paper, and the monotonous roar of the room heater that struggled to blow enough warm air to keep the freezing outdoor temperatures from seeping through the thin walls.

Snippets of their previous conversation ran through Justin's mind. He shook his head, certain he would never understand the female thought processes.

But whatever she'd been thinking about the two of them sharing this room, she was apparently okay with it. Again. Or still. Or whatever.

Because she thought he didn't want her anymore?

Fat chance of that. The way he felt right then, he'd still be wanting her when he was ninety.

Want, but not necessarily understand. Who could understand a woman who would run, literally, half the length of the damn state, to avoid talking about marriage, then calmly share a motel room with one bed with the same man she'd been running from.

Across the room, on the far side of the bed, Blaire was not asleep. From the moment she had lain down she had heard every breath Justin had taken, every creak of the chair as he had shifted his weight, every rustle of his newspaper.

Now she heard him fold the paper and set it aside. She felt his gaze travel over her, from the back of her head, down her shoulders, her back, her legs.

She wished she had pulled the bedspread over herself. Had she done so, she wouldn't now feel quite so exposed.

She wondered what he was thinking, sitting over there staring at her. He was probably shaking his head, thinking she'd lost her mind, running from him in the morning, sharing a motel room that afternoon.

In truth, she didn't know what she was doing. Maybe pregnancy really did make a woman stupid. It would be nice to be able to blame it all on raging hormones.

In her case, however, it was due more to her own insecurities than hormones. At least, she thought so.

When the subject of marriage arose, she panicked. Marriage terrified her. She was so afraid of ending up like her parents that running to Enid, then Ponca City, then Stillwater, then heading for home just to keep some sort of distance between her and Justin made perfect sense.

So did sharing a motel room with that same man.

Go figure.

They'd already shared a motel room, she was already pregnant. Nothing else bad could happen.

Not that she thought of being pregnant as bad! Unplanned or not, she wanted this baby, welcomed it with her whole heart.

She was utterly comfortable sharing a room with Justin. She was completely uncomfortable discussing marriage.

There. That made perfect sense to her.

Behind her she heard Justin rise and walk to the bed. The mattress dipped with his weight. It took him a minute to tug off his boots, then she felt him stretch out beside her.

She concentrated on remaining relaxed. He thought she was asleep. If she tensed up he would know she was faking it. That would be too embarrassing.

A few minutes later his breathing grew deep and even. He was asleep.

Or he was faking it, as she was. She smiled at the thought of the two of them sharing a bed and pretending to sleep.

That was not what they'd done the last time they'd shared a bed. Nobody had faked anything that night.

At the memory, a deep warmth rushed through her and settled between her legs. It was all she could do to swallow the moan that threatened.

He wasn't even touching her. She couldn't even see him. Yet still, she wanted him in the worst way. She wanted to feel his hands, hard and callused from work, on her bare flesh. Wanted to feel his warm, naked skin, surprisingly smooth, beneath her fingers. She wanted to taste him, smell him, take him inside and hold him there as he filled her so that she felt as if she would never feel alone again.

She let herself drift on images of him until she imagined she lay facing him and could feel the hard dips and bulges of the muscles in his arms and shoulders beneath her hands. The warmth of him drew her closer. The breadth of his chest invited her to snuggle.

Oh, it felt so good to be close to him this way, even if it was only in her imagination.

She let herself drift further, until she imagined his arms surrounding her, pulling her flush against him. His heat was incredible, and yet she knew the two of them would generate more, until they both went up in flames.

She wanted that. That mindless pleasure, the likes of which she had felt with no other man.

Sure, she'd had orgasms before, but none so sharp and intense as when she was with Justin.

His hand slid around her ribs and up to cup one breast.

Ahh. Such warmth, such pleasure. Then she pictured his thumb flicking across her nipple and she whimpered. Even in her imagination she felt the sharp pull of pleasure reach down to the core of her and make her squirm.

She wanted to feel his flesh, but there was fabric in her way. A shirt. Why was he wearing a shirt?

With nimble fingers she unbuttoned several buttons until she could slide her hands inside and feel his chest muscles flex under her touch.

She wanted to taste him. She stretched up and started at his neck. With lips and tongue and teeth, she indulged herself. Never had her imagination been so real. She could swear she tasted the slight salty flavor of his skin, and farther up, over his jaw and onto his cheek, the slight rasp of a day's worth of whisker growth. She loved his whiskers, the way they rasped against her hand, the way they made her lips tingle.

She wanted better access. She pushed him onto his back and straddled his hips. This was her fantasy, wasn't it? She could do whatever she wanted.

But when she leaned forward to kiss him, his hands pressed against her shoulders and stopped her.

"Blaire?"

Blaire blinked and looked down in shock. Justin lay beneath her while she straddled his hips. One of her hands was inside his unbuttoned shirt. His chest was heaving. Her loins were throbbing. Her nipples were erect and hard.

"Oh, Justin!"

"It's all right."

"No! I'm sorry." She tried to scramble off of him and away, but couldn't seem to move. "I didn't—"

"Shh." He placed a forefinger across her lips. "Look at me. Blaire, look at me."

Realizing she had her eyes squeezed shut, Blaire forced herself to open them and look at him.

"It seems to me," he said, tugging on her arms to pull her down to his chest, "that you and I were having the same dream."

She saw it then, in his dark brown eyes. That look of heat, of passion. Of a man's attention focused solely and intently upon one certain woman.

It was a look that took her breath away. He pulled her down until her breasts met his chest. The same chest she had bared and run her hands across in her imagination. In her sleep.

The most natural place for her mouth to settle was against his.

"Justin," she said on a sigh.

Their lips met with an explosion of soft heat. Blaire felt every bone melt right there inside her own body. It had been weeks since she'd been this close to him, kissed him, tasted his heat, felt his hands on her.

How she had missed being with him this way.

Was that the same as missing the man? She feared it was. There was so much more to him than simply a great lover, but in that particular moment, she put it all aside and enjoyed. She might never have a chance to be with him again this way, so she would take advantage of it while she could.

His lips were soft yet firm, hot and slick. His tongue dove into her mouth and danced with hers. She tasted salt, and coffee, and Justin. With a moan, she deepened the kiss.

With an answering moan Justin wrapped his arms around her and rolled until Blaire lay on her back and Justin lay nestled right where he'd longed to be for weeks and weeks, in the cradle of her thighs.

"Let me," he whispered against her mouth. He reached between them for the snap on her jeans. But he didn't free it. He raised his head, breaking their kiss, and waited until she looked at him with eyes of liquid golden brown. "Let me," he asked again.

Blaire didn't give him a verbal answer. Instead she used one hand to pull his head down again until their lips met. With the other she helped him unsnap and unzip her jeans.

It was answer enough for Justin. Within seconds he had her jeans opened and his hand cupping the heat of her, nothing separating him from the core of her but a thin layer of silk.

At his touch Blaire's hips rose. With a gasp she thrust herself hard into his hand. Oh, she had missed this. Missed the way he touched her, the way he could drive her to the brink so easily. Their one night together had not been nearly enough.

Their last time together, they had liked each other, certainly. But mostly they'd been driven by hot blood and hormones.

This time, she knew him a little better, and what she knew made her want him more, made her care about him more. Was she in love with him?

He removed his hand from between her legs.

Blaire moaned in protest, forgetting entirely her emotional dilemma in favor of the more pressing physical one: whether or not to lay back and beg for his touch, or reverse their positions, straddle his hips as she had done earlier, and take what she wanted from him.

Justin didn't give her time to make a decision, had her mind been capable of such a feat just then. He pulled the bottom edge of her sweater up and over her head, forcing her arms upward in the process. And he left her that way, with her arms stretched over her head, trapped in the sleeves of her sweater.

She began to struggle to free her arms. She wanted them wrapped around him, wanted her hands on him, not all tangled up in a sweater.

Justin stilled her with his hands on her arms. It wasn't his gentle touch that caused her to cease her struggles as much as it was the look in his eyes. A smile lurked there, a devilish one, along with heat and a promise of more pleasurable things to come.

"Be still," he whispered, "and let me."

Blaire's heart raced. "Let you what?"

He leaned down and flicked his tongue along the upper edge of her bra. "Do anything I want."

Blaire sucked in a sharp breath. Flames of anticipation teased her from nipple to loins and back again. "I guess," she managed, her lungs suddenly struggling for air, "that would depend on what you want."

He smiled slowly. "For starters…" With the fingers of one hand he flipped open the catch on her front-closure bra. He dipped his head and took one nipple gently between his teeth.

Blaire sucked in another sharp breath. Her breast seemed to swell to meet his mouth.

His teeth teased and nipped almost, but not quite,

to the point of pain. His lips and tongue joined in and drove her so wild that she cried out and arched her back clear off the bed.

Her reaction drove Justin closer to the edge of control than he wanted to be. He didn't want to rush this. He knew she wanted him, but when her brain kicked into gear again she was going to come up with all sorts of reasons why they shouldn't do this.

When she did, he was going to have to come up with answering reasons why they should. Why they should love each other. Why they should get married. Why they should raise their baby together.

Baby. The two of them had already made a baby together. The breast beneath his lips would nourish that child through infancy. Was it his imagination, or was it already fuller than it had been, in anticipation of the new life it must feed? Women's breasts became more sensitive during pregnancy, didn't they? He thought he'd read that somewhere.

He raised his head and looked at Blaire. "Am I hurting you?"

Blaire blinked. "What?"

He cupped her breast in his palm. "Your breast. I was wondering if you're more sensitive here, if maybe I was being too rough."

Blaire's heart turned over in her chest. "No." Her vision blurred. "You weren't hurting me. Except by stopping."

He grinned. "Liked it, did you?"

Blaire studied the ceiling and shrugged. "It was all right."

"That's all?" He leaned down and swiped his tongue across her nipple again.

Blaire could not hold back another sharp breath.

Justin chuckled. "That's what I thought." He kissed his way down her breastbone and into the vee of her unzipped jeans. He pressed his lips against her yellow panties and blew hot air through them and onto her skin.

"Hear that, kid? Your mom's a big fibber."

In that instant when he spoke to their child snuggled safely in her womb, Blaire felt a connection snap into place in the vicinity of her heart. Until right then, she was the only person alive to ever speak to the baby, to acknowledge that it was a real person. Now there were two of them.

Blaire knew she was suddenly in serious trouble. She might have been able to resist, had Justin not spoken to the baby, but he had. She was a goner. If she'd had doubts before—and she had—they were gone. Whisked away by a few simple words spoken by a man she wanted to trust but didn't know how.

Yet her inability to trust didn't seem to matter to her heart. She had just fallen totally, completely in love with the father of her child.

Chapter Nine

Justin looked up and saw not laughter in her eyes, but some other deeper emotion. It filled her eyes and glowed from her face and made something inside him go all soft and tender, even while another part of him hardened.

He couldn't take his gaze from hers. Clothes that should have required effort to remove seemed to fall away with ease, then they lay together, flesh on flesh, muscle to muscle, chest to breast, hip to hip. Breath to breath.

Blaire raised her knees to make more room for him, to grip his hips and hold him close to her.

Wordlessly Justin accepted the invitation. He

joined his hands with hers, and then his body, entering her slowly, one hot, slick inch at a time.

Blaire felt him stretch her, fill her. It was as if she was being completed, made whole when she hadn't realized any part of her had been missing. She welcomed him inside, urged him to go deeper. Slowly at first, until slow was no longer sufficient to ease the terrible wanting that consumed her. Then faster, harder. She met him thrust for thrust, knowing that in the end he would hold her and they would fly off the edge of the earth together.

And they did.

The first thing Blaire became aware of minutes later was the heat and pressure of Justin's glorious weight covering her as if shielding her from the cold, cold wind howling outside their door.

Justin was also aware of his weight and feared he might be crushing Blaire or the baby or both. As the strength returned to his limbs he pushed himself up on his arms and started to shift his weight off her.

Blaire made a tiny sound of protest in the back of her throat. It was about all she was capable of at the moment. She wanted to raise her arms and hold him there, but her arms were too limp. But she did manage to press her knees against his hips.

"No," she whispered. "Don't go. Not yet."

Justin eased his weight onto his elbows. "How is

it," he asked, cupping her face in his hands, "that you and I are so damn good together?"

"Luck?" she answered.

He shook his head and kissed the tip of her nose. "Fate."

"You believe in fate?"

"I believe some things are meant to be," he said quietly. "Don't you?"

Blaire found that she could no longer meet his gaze. "I believe the conversation is turning a little more serious than I'd like."

Justin gave her a quick smile. "Coward."

"That's me."

"It is not," he objected. "But I'll let you off the hook anyway."

They got dressed and spent the rest of the day watching old movies on television. Blaire might have felt awkward—she expected to, after their love-making—but Justin proved so easy to be with that awkwardness was impossible. Throughout their movie-watching they argued about the on-screen action, debated the merits of different characters, cracked jokes about all of it, then eventually they got hungry again. The snow was deeper than it had been by a couple of inches.

"Why don't you stay here and I'll bring our dinner back to the room?" Justin suggested.

"Because the food would freeze before you got

back with it. I vote we bundle up and walk." Blaire peeked out between the edges of the drapes. "The parking lot's pretty full, and I bet it's slicker than glass."

"Meaning you think I'll run into something if we drive?"

"Well, no offense, but…"

He laughed. "None taken. Under these conditions, walking would be safer. But it's damn cold out there. I don't see any reason for you to freeze your tush off. They can wrap the food so it won't get cold in the few minutes it'll take me to get back with it."

Blaire crossed her arms and pursed her lips. "If you think I'm going to sit here all snug and warm and play the little woman while the big, bad man forges his way out into the wilderness in a blizzard to bring me something to eat, you're sadly mistaken."

"Aw, come on." He gave her a look that said she was being unreasonable.

Blaire objected to that look. She objected to his making decisions for her. She objected to his assuming she would simply go along with him, stay when he said stay, come when he said come.

And she thought she loved him?

"It's freezing out there," he protested with a wave of his hand toward the door. "Why do you want to go out in that?"

"I don't, particularly, but I'm hungry, and I want

out of this room for a while. If that means wading through snow in a blizzard, then that's what I'll do."

With a scowl on his face, Justin pulled her coat from its hanger and held it. "I suppose if I try to help you on with your coat I'll hear all about how you've been putting on your own coat all your life and don't need help now."

"See there?" She beamed at him. "We're getting to know each other real well."

He tossed her coat to her and grabbed his own. "Have you always been this stubborn?"

"Yes." She slipped her arms into her coat. "But if you want to offer to bring me food and run my errands in a few months when I'm big and fat I probably won't be."

The thought of her big and fat, because of his child, made him pause with his coat half on. He shook his head as if to clear it. "I can't picture it."

"Picture what? Me fat?"

"That, and agreeable," he said.

"Oh, you." She snatched a pillow from the bed and threw it at him.

With a laugh, Justin ducked and threw his arm up. The pillow bounced harmlessly back to the bed.

When they stepped from their cozy motel room into the blizzard, the wind was so sharp and cold it sucked the tears right out of their eyes. Out in the parking lot they sank past their ankles in snow. For Justin, in his boots, it was no problem as long as it wasn't too slick. But Blaire had on sneakers. Cotton socks were all that protected her ankles. She walked as fast as she could to lessen the duration of her exposure.

The world they traipsed through was nothing more than a swirling whiteness lined on either side with glowing street lights and the occasional set of headlights creeping past at a slow pace.

The restaurant, when they stepped inside after traipsing the fifty yards from their room, was a sharp contrast of light, loud voices, and heat that seemed excessive.

Justin and Blaire took their time ordering, and eating, neither in a hurry to return and lock themselves away in their motel room again too soon.

But they couldn't dawdle forever, so eventually they made their way back.

"Is the wind dying down?" she asked when they were about halfway back to the motel. "Or is that just wishful thinking on my part?"

"No," Justin said, sticking his nose into the air. "I think you're right."

"Here's hoping it's not just a temporary lull," she said, huddling down farther into her coat.

"Dare I say you could have stayed in the room?"

"Depends on how lucky you're feeling," she told him, grateful they didn't have far to go but not willing to admit it.

"Oh," was all he said. But he smiled when he said it.

The room they had so eagerly left no more than an hour earlier now looked welcoming to them.

They had left the lamp and television on, a habit Justin had developed long ago. He felt that if anyone was up to no good and snooping around, hearing the television would probably send them off to find a quieter, darker room to break into.

Now Justin opened the door and ushered Blaire inside. "Home at last," he said.

Blaire smirked. "I wouldn't go that far, but at least now I can take my shoes off."

"Your feet must be frozen."

"If you say so." She hung up her coat, then toed off her sneakers. "I can't feel them enough to tell."

Instantly concerned—as if he hadn't been worried enough about her all evening—Justin hung his coat beside hers. As soon as he'd tugged off his boots—not an easy task without a bootjack—he made her sit on the bed. He drew the chair up and sat before her.

"Give me your feet."

Blaire blinked. "What?"

"Your feet." He patted his thighs. "Put 'em here. I'll warm them."

"Now there's an offer I'll take you up on." Blaire sat on the edge of the bed and placed one foot on Justin's thigh. "If I give you both feet I'll fall over backward."

"And your point is?"

Blaire laughed. "Okay. Since I ate like a pig,

stretching out sounds inviting." She leaned back and braced herself on both elbows and gave him her stockinged feet.

Justin pressed the bottoms of her feet against his abdomen and rubbed the tops with both his hands.

It took only a few seconds before Blaire felt the heat seep through her socks and into her icy skin.

She moaned in relief. "Oh, that feels good."

"I'm glad you like it." He rubbed vigorously until his hands felt hot. Then slowly he pulled off one sock and held her bare foot in his hands.

It was so damned small, Justin thought, and pale compared to his hands. Just like the entire woman. Dainty and white, while he was…not. He was a big man, dark skinned, not particularly graceful except when on horseback. Not that men should be graceful, but she was, and her grace simply emphasized what a big, clumsy clod he was.

Hell, maybe she was right. Maybe they had no business getting married. What did he know about raising a child? Guiding another human being from infancy to adulthood and have them turn out to be not only a productive member of society, but a genuinely good person. Because that's what he wanted for this child of theirs, that he or she be, above all else, a genuinely good person.

For that matter, what did Blaire know of raising children? Surely no more than he did, except women seemed to be born with some secret well of knowledge about children. Sort of like men being born understanding car engines and electrical wiring. It was genetic.

And that was bull.

Besides, marriage was first and foremost about a man and a woman and their commitment to each other. Children, even ones who were already on the way, came after the making of that commitment. At least, that was the way Justin thought things should go. For it to work and last, the marriage and commitment had to be genuine for their own sakes, not merely for the sake of the child.

Didn't they?

God help him, how was a man supposed to know what to do? Why didn't Blaire seem to be struggling with this subject? She seemed to know exactly how she wanted things to go, and her plans didn't include him.

Maybe she knew better than he did, but Justin wasn't ready to accept that. Never mind that he wasn't sure how to do what needed to be done. He knew what was right. He knew what needed to be.

He would have to rethink his strategy. He had to find a way around her reluctance.

First, he would warm her feet. Then he would decide what came next.

He removed her other sock.

Blaire closed her eyes in relief and pleasure. His warm, strong hand enveloped her cold foot and sent heat seeping through her toes and up her leg.

Who knew, she wondered as the heat rose farther and farther up her leg, that a foot could be an erogenous zone?

She opened her eyes to see if he realized what he was doing to her and knew instantly that his mind was a million miles away. And then he blinked, and his gaze focused on her like a laser targeting its mark. A deep shiver wracked her. She felt his hot gaze over every inch of her.

With their gazes locked, he pulled his shirttail from the waist of his jeans and tucked her feet underneath, pressing her bare soles directly against his bare abdomen.

It was impossible to say who sucked in the deeper breath, as they both gasped at the contact. And not merely because her feet were cool and his flesh was hot.

Justin rubbed the tops of her feet, then stroked them with his fingertips. Then he stroked up to her ankles, and up beneath the hem of her jeans until he couldn't reach any farther.

"Are your legs cold?" he asked, his voice low and rough, their gazes still locked.

"Do I get to rub them against your skin if they are?"

A slow smile curved his lips. "Is that what you want to do?"

"My legs," she offered, reaching for the zipper of her jeans, "are freezing."

"Well, then." Justin reached up and helped her tug down her jeans. "We can't have you being cold."

"Nor you." She reached for his shoulders and urged him onto the bed with her. "That's better."

In sharp contrast to the fast-paced action adventure movie on the television, Blaire and Justin moved together as if performing a slow ballet, one graceful motion at a time, first by her, then him. Hands stroked, lips tasted, clothes drifted away one article at a time.

There was no cold flesh, as heat moved from him through her and back again.

There was no hurry, no rush to reach that peak of pleasure. They knew it was there, waiting for them. They knew it would be all the sweeter for taking their time in getting there.

On the television, tires screeched and bullets exploded from guns.

On the bed, breaths held in pleasure, then came out in soft sighs. Touches lingered, gazes smiled.

When Justin entered her Blaire felt her own completion in the most profound way. This was right, the two of them together, with the child they created between them.

Her vision blurred. His name left her lips softly, with deep emotion.

Justin was humbled by the tears in her eyes and the depth of emotion in her voice. For his part, he felt as if he had finally come home, there in her arms. He had felt this way only three times in his life. Every one of those times had been when he was buried deep inside this one woman.

He knew that had to mean that they were meant to be together, but just then he couldn't concentrate enough to turn the thought over in his mind. The pressure in his loins was building, and Blaire was urging him faster, harder, deeper.

Together they climbed that steep slope and slid quietly yet unmistakably over the edge into the mindless world of colors and breathless wonder.

They slept that night in each other's arms, flesh to flesh, heart to heart. Four times, now, they had made love, and they had napped together earlier that very day. But they had never fallen asleep in each other's arms, knowing they need not wake until morning. It was a luxury and a gift, and Blaire closed her eyes and reveled in it.

Justin woke once to turn off the light and television. So much, he thought with a smile, for Blaire's belief that she could only sleep in the dark and quiet.

Outside the wind had died. He lifted one edge of the drapes and peered out, noting that the snow had finally stopped, leaving everything covered in a thick blanket of white.

When he crawled back beneath the covers, Blaire's arms welcomed him, even while she slept.

Now that, he thought, had to mean something. In her sleep she wanted him, trusted him, welcomed him. Surely she could learn to do those things when awake, couldn't she?

He tried to wrap his mind around a way to make her want to marry him, but he felt so loose and re-laxed that he found he couldn't string two coherent thoughts together. Within minutes he was once again asleep.

When Justin opened his eyes, Blaire was staring at him with a bemused smile. There was enough light seeping in around the edges of the drapes across the room behind him that he knew it was daylight.

"Good morning." He gave her a smile of his own. "I could get used to this, waking up with you. I think you should change your mind and marry me."

A funny look crossed her face. Her lips mashed tightly together, her eyes widened, and her cheeks bellowed. Her skin looked a little on the green side.

"Blaire?"

She slapped one hand over her mouth, made a strangling noise, and leaped from the bed and toward the bathroom. A second later Justin heard the clank of the toilet lid being thrown back and the unmistak-able sound of a woman tossing her cookies.

Alarmed, he dashed after her, feeling more help-less than he could remember ever feeling. All he could do was kneel at her side and hold her hair back and away from her face. He nearly got sick himself watch-ing her heave into the commode again and again.

Finally she sat back on her heels, eyes closed, and panted.

Hurriedly Justin wet a washcloth at the sink and wiped her face. "Hell, darlin', if you didn't want to marry me, a simple no would have done it."

Blaire, still a little nauseated, more than a little humiliated at having him witness her throwing up her guts, took the washcloth from him and covered her face with it in time to muffle a burst of laughter. "Don't be silly."

Then, in an abrupt turnaround of mood familiar to pregnant women everywhere, she burst into tears.

"Aw, come on, honey, don't cry." He started to take her in his arms, but she sucked in a sharp breath and made another dive for the toilet.

Nothing came up this time, for which Justin was grateful. He wasn't sure how much more he could take without dropping to his knees and joining her.

After another few minutes, when Blaire felt steady enough, Justin helped her back to bed. He smoothed the covers over her shoulders and kissed her nose. "What else can I do? What do you need?"

Blaire sniffed. "You're being awfully sweet about this."

"Why wouldn't I be? I assume this is morning sickness caused by the baby, but even if it wasn't, you can't help it if you're sick. I've been sick a time or two. I always like somebody to lend me a hand. Do you want some water?"

She rolled her head slightly from side to side on the pillow. "Crackers. In my coat pocket."

"You carry crackers in your coat?" He reached into the pocket of her coat and came up with a cellophane package containing two saltine crackers.

"They came with my salad," she explained at his questioning look.

"Is this enough?" He tore open the package and gave her a cracker. "Just these two little crackers? I can get you more."

Nibbling on the cracker, Blaire smiled. "I won't need more, at least until tomorrow morning."

Justin shuddered to think of having to go through, day after day, what she'd just gone through. "Does it happen every day?"

"Almost," she said, reaching for the second cracker. "But it goes away pretty fast."

"That's something," he said. "I guess. How long is this supposed to last?"

She shrugged. "It's different for every woman. But with any luck it should go away in another few weeks."

"Weeks?" He felt his stomach turn over at the very thought.

She finished her cracker and traced a finger across his cheek. "It's sweet of you to care."

"Care? It's our baby that's making you sick. Of course I care. And I meant what I said earlier. I do wish you'd change your mind and marry me."

She smiled up at him sadly. "Are you in love with me, Justin?"

Her question startled him. Had she been reading his thoughts from the day before? "I…"

"Don't you think we should be in love with each other before we get married?" she asked.

Dammit, she was making his own argument for him. Now he had to argue the other side.

"I admit," he said slowly, "that that's how it should be, but we've kinda put things out of order, you and I. And anyway, I don't know if I even know what love is. I've never been in love before, Blaire. I know I feel things for you I've never felt for another woman, but is it love? I suppose I could lie and say yes, but I can't lie to you. The God's honest truth is, I don't know."

Blaire swallowed a hard knot of disappointment. She shouldn't have been surprised; she'd known he wasn't in love with her. Just because she loved him didn't mean he had to return her feelings.

"We could still make a go of it," he said.

"A go of it?" She felt dazed, bruised. Heaven help her, had she harbored some hope that they would fall into each other's arms and swear their undying love for each other?

Nonsense. She pushed herself up and leaned against the headboard, tucking the sheet beneath her arms.

"Yeah," Justin said. "I mean, just because we're not madly in love doesn't meant we can't make it work. As long as we respect each other's feelings, and we're polite and honest and considerate with each other, how many problems could we have that we couldn't see through?"

She was shaking her head no before he finished speaking. Probably, she thought, because his words made such uncommonly good sense for two people in their situation.

"Surely we could get through the next few months, until the baby's born, without doing any lasting damage to each other," he offered. "If we're not happy with each other by then, we can go our separate ways. Meanwhile the baby carries the Chisholm name and the two of you get taken care of and don't have to worry about the future."

"Justin, I'm honored that you want to marry me, honest I am. But I told myself a long, long time ago that I would marry for love—mutual love—or not at all. I won't try to cut you out of the baby's life, and I won't turn down your help—when I need help. But none of that means we need to get married."

Justin scrubbed a hand over his face in frustration. "I'll ask again," he warned.

"Not for a while, please," she said. "Just let it go for a few weeks. Please?"

Justin let out a long breath. "All right. If that's the way you want it. But I can't keep this from my family for much longer."

"No," she said. "That's no fair. My family knows. There's no reason you can't tell yours."

"You don't mind?"

"No. They're the baby's family, too."

"Do you want to be there when I tell them?"

She gave him a crooked smile. "At the risk of proving what a coward I am, no. If we were announcing that we were getting married—"

"Fine by me."

"—that would be different. But since we're not, I'll let you tell them without me."

"They'll probably all show up at the feed store, one at a time, to see you."

She nodded and stared at her hands in her lap. "I'll be ready."

Justin laughed and used one forefinger to nudge her chin up so she would look at him. "They wouldn't be coming to point fingers and make faces. They'll be coming to see how you're doing, if you need anything. They'll probably start bringing baby presents the day after I tell them."

"Oh, they wouldn't."

"They would, and neither you nor I will be able to stop them, especially my grandmother. This will be the birth of her first great-grandchild, so brace yourself."

By noon Justin had sat still in the motel for as long as he could. The storm was gone, the sun was shining, the snow was melting rapidly, especially on the roads.

Still, he wouldn't take chances with Blaire's safety. He waited another couple of hours to let the traffic and the highway department do the work of clearing the roads.

He called a local garage and arranged to have Blaire's car towed in and checked out. They promised not to do any actual repairs without her permission.

"As soon as it's drivable," Justin told Blaire, "I'll drive you back up here to get it."

Blaire merely hummed, not disagreeing, but not specifically agreeing, either. She had agreed to accept his help, but only when she needed it. Her mother was more than capable of driving Blaire to Stillwater to get her car. Her father was certainly able, if not particularly willing, to handle the store without either of them for a few hours.

It was with relief that she joined Justin in the cab of his pickup for the drive home.

At least, she told herself it was relief. But she would probably dream for the next month about falling asleep and waking up in his arms. About his tender care of her when the morning sickness hit. About his thought-provoking solution to marriage when there was no deep love.

The roads were already mostly clear, but snow-packed and icy patches waited to send the careless off into the nearest ditch. A few miles out of town that was where she spotted her little red car—in the ditch. It was only identifiable because the sun had melted the snow enough that the red roof of the car was exposed.

She hoped the car would be all right until it was towed to safety.

Then she faced forward, and looked toward home. It was time to get back to reality.

Chapter Ten

The reality Blaire returned to was anything but pleasant.

Everything was fine when Justin pulled up at her garage apartment and carried her things upstairs for her. He didn't stay. She didn't ask him to. Somehow on the way home the silence between them became less and less comfortable until the air in the cab felt thick with tension.

Still, their parting was friendly enough. And she did remember to thank him for rescuing her from the ditch, and for taking care of her when she'd been sick that morning.

"You don't need to thank me," he'd protested.

"Maybe not, but I do anyway," she told him. "Will

you let me know how it goes when you tell your family about the baby?"

"Sure." He smiled and brushed a finger down her cheek. "But there's not going to be a problem, as long as they know I've asked you to marry me," he added.

Blaire stared at him. "Is that why you've been asking? Because your family will expect it?"

"If you think insulting me will get me to stop asking, you're sadly mistaken."

"I wasn't insulting you," she protested. "I was seeking information."

"Your question was insulting. I've been asking you to marry me because I want to marry you. For me. For myself. And for the baby. The rest of my family has nothing to do with it, and no say in the matter."

"You'll explain that to them, won't you?"

"Yes." He gave her a sharp nod. "I will."

Okay, Blaire thought when he drove off a moment later. That could have gone better.

Before she could stew about it or even cry, which was what she wanted most to do, she squared her shoulders and headed for her office in her parents' house. Her mother'd had to handle the books—which, after all, had always been her job anyway until she broke her arm last summer—for several days in a row. She was probably ready to chew nails.

Yet when Blaire entered the house she found her mother sitting on the couch in the living room, with her feet up, watching a soap opera.

"You're home," she said, her face registering surprise when Blaire walked into the room.

"I called and said I was on the way."

"I know, sweetie, I just didn't expect you so soon. So, tell me." Using the remote, she turned off the television and patted the spot beside her on the sofa. "How did it go?"

Blaire shrugged and took the offered seat. "It went great, until the blizzard. I got to see Connie and Sherry, but Gayle wasn't home. I know, I know." She held up a hand to forestall anything her mother might say. "If I had called first I would have known that. But I had a good time visiting with Sherry and Connie, anyway."

Nancy Harding tsked and shook her head. "You never used to be so dense, dear. When I asked how it went, I meant with you and Justin."

Blaire narrowed her eyes. "Oh, yes, you're the one who told him where I was and how to find me."

"And?" her mother asked expectantly.

"And, what?" If her mother wanted information, Blaire was going to make her work for it.

"You know 'and what.' What happened when he found you? Are you getting married?"

"Mother, I've told you before, Justin and I are not getting married."

"But he asked you, didn't he?"

"He did. And yes, I said no."

"But, why?" Her mother looked truly baffled.

Blaire, however, was the baffled one. "How can you ask that? I've told you and told you that I will never willingly put myself in a position to end up with a marriage like yours and Daddy's. The two of you bicker and snipe at each other all the time. I don't want to live that way."

Her mother popped up off the sofa as if on springs. "Now you listen here, young lady. I'm getting sick and tired of your constantly criticizing our marriage. It's not your place to approve or disapprove how your father and I are with each other."

Blaire closed her eyes and turned her head away. "I know that. I'm sorry, Mama." Taking in a deep breath, she faced her mother. "I know it's not my place, and I don't say these things to hurt you or make you angry. But I see how unhappy you both are so much of the time, and now you're telling me I need to make the same bed for myself."

"Seems to me, missy, you already did make the same bed for yourself. Made it, spent some time rolling around in it, if your condition is anything to go by."

"Mama!"

"Well? You feel so free to criticize me and my marriage, I'm just laying out the truth for you to see with your own eyes."

Blaire groaned and pushed herself up from the sofa. "This is getting us nowhere. I came over to check on the bookkeeping."

"Fortunately for you, but not your father, business

has been slow because of the snow. The books are all up to date and ready for you to take over. And while I'm standing here glancing out the window," she added with a frown, "where's your car?"

Oops. "Uh, well, it's kinda…"

"Oh, I know that look," her mother said. "What have you done? Where is your car?"

"All right. It's in a ditch a few miles outside Stillwater."

"A *ditch?*" her mother shrieked. "How bad was it? Were you hurt? Are you all right? The baby?"

"We're fine." It warmed Blaire's heart that her mother seemed to care so much about the baby. "Both of us. I slid off the road in the blizzard and slid down an embankment into the ditch. It was no big deal, except I couldn't get out. Justin helped me, and my car's being towed to a body shop as soon as the tow truck can get it out."

Her mother pursed her lips and crossed her arms, a calculating look coming into her eyes. "You ran off the road during the blizzard."

"That's right. What are you getting at?"

"When did this happen?"

"Yesterday morning, when the blizzard hit. Why are you looking at me that way?"

"What way?"

"Like you think I'm holding out on you or something."

"Aren't you? Justin rescued you yesterday?"

"That's right."

"And where have you and he been since then?"

Blaire rolled her eyes toward the ceiling. "Oh, Mama, give it a rest. Just because we shared the last available motel room in Stillwater—because it was too dangerous to travel—doesn't mean a thing."

"I'll tell you what it means," her mother said sharply. "If you're not interested in marrying the man, you should at least stop sleeping with him. Otherwise, somebody—like maybe Justin himself—is going to get the idea that you think he's good enough to sleep with but not good enough to marry."

"Mama! What a terrible thing to say."

"You mean that's not the way it is?"

"Of course not."

"If you say so," her mother told her. "If you say so, sweetie. In which case, I'm afraid your father and I are going to have to insist that you and Justin get married."

Blaire blinked. "I beg your pardon."

"It's the only right thing to do. For you and for the baby. You have to think about the baby, Blaire, and not just yourself, you know. It's time to grow up and face the consequences of your actions."

Blaire swallowed against a knot of bitterness in her throat. "Is that what I've been to you? The consequences of your actions?"

"Don't sass me, young lady."

"You tell me to act like an adult, yet I'm supposed to be an obedient child and do as I'm told. You can't have it both ways, Mama. If I'm an adult, and I assure you I am, then I make my own decisions."

Her mother's face stiffened. "As long as you're living under our roof—"

"Now wait just a minute. You can't pull out that old trick. First of all, I live over the garage, and the apartment is part of the pitifully low salary the store pays me since you broke your arm. I gave up my apartment, my job, my life, to come home and help you around the house and Daddy around the store. If I'm living under your roof, it's because you've asked me to."

"That's right. Throw my injury in my face."

"Mama," Blaire wailed. It was going to be a long, long night.

Justin didn't have time to wonder how Blaire's homecoming with her parents was going; he had his own family to deal with. He called a last-minute family meeting for supper that night. It was the only way to assure that Caleb and Melanie would come.

A dinner invitation could be declined. Notice of a family meeting could not.

"What's this all about, Justin?" Caleb asked when he and his bride of fewer than three months arrived.

Justin cut his gaze toward Sloan's stepdaughters, Janie and Libby, then back to Caleb. "Can't a guy want to see his brother—not to mention his newest sister-in-law—without everybody getting so suspicious?"

Caleb caught on immediately to the fact that Justin didn't want to talk about the purpose of the meeting in front of the two young girls.

"So." He punched Justin in the shoulder. "Trying to make time with my wife, huh?"

"Hey," Justin protested. "You think I'm stupid? I only do that when you're not around, not when I've invited you to supper."

"Yeah." Melanie rubbed her husband's arm and smiled up at him. "He only tries to make time with me when you're not around."

Caleb rolled his eyes and snorted. "Never mind. Forget I said anything."

Justin smirked. "I usually do."

After supper, while Pedro took care of some final chores out in the barn, Maria asked Janie and Libby to help her with baby Rosa. The request was a sure-fire guarantee that the two little girls would be busy for some time, since they both adored Rosa.

The rest of the family gathered in the living room.

"Now," Rose said firmly. "Perhaps Justin will tell us what this is all about?"

"Yes, Grandmother." Justin shuffled his feet a time or two and stuck his hands into his back pockets while trying not to look anyone in the eye.

"What have you done?" Sloan demanded.

Justin frowned. "What?"

"You're acting guilty as hell about something," Sloan said. "Come on, just tell us. It can't be that bad."

"No," Justin protested. "It's not bad. At least, not as far as I'm concerned. To me it's good news. Great news. The best—"

"Then tell us what it is," Caleb snapped.

"Yes, Justin, please do." Rose smiled quietly. "Some of us don't have as much time left on this earth as others."

"Oh, very funny, Grandmother," he said. "But I think you've got enough time left to be here when my son or daughter is born next September."

The silence that fell across the room was complete and thick.

Finally Rose nodded slowly. "So this is what has been on your mind these past many weeks."

"Actually," he admitted, "I've only known about it for a couple of weeks."

"And are you going to tell us who the mother of your child is?"

"Blaire Harding."

Cherokee Rose Chisholm felt her heart swell. There was pride and love in her youngest grandson's voice when he spoke the name of the woman who carried his child. No one could ask for more than that. Justin was a good boy, a good man, with a heart as big as the world.

"I assume there's a wedding in the planning?" she said.

"Uh, well…"

Sloan straightened away from the wall he'd been

leaning against. A hard light came into his eyes. "Don't tell me you're not going to marry her."

"It's more like she won't marry me," Justin countered with no small amount of self-disgust. "But I'm working on her."

"You do that," Sloan said. "Just see that you do that very thing."

"Now, Sloan." His wife, Emily, patted his arm and gave Justin an encouraging smile. "You know Justin will do his best. Blaire will come around once she realizes what a terrific guy he is."

"Is that the problem?" Melanie doubled her fists and frowned. "She doesn't think you're terrific? Where is she. Give me five minutes alone with her—"

"Pardon me," Justin said to Caleb. Then he grabbed Melanie and planted a big, sloppy kiss right on her mouth, while she was still talking.

Melanie sputtered into silence, albeit a short-lived one. "Well, hell. Isn't that just like you? I've known you my entire life, and you wait until *after* I marry your brother before you kiss me. No wonder Blaire won't marry you. You're an idiot."

Feeling as if his wife had effectively put his little brother in his proper place, Caleb folded his arms across his chest and smiled.

Justin raised his eyes to the ceiling as if seeking help. Then he shook his head. "Blaire has said that she doesn't want to get married, but that she has no intention of keeping me out of the baby's life. Before any of you say anything, yes, I plan to do my best to change her mind about marrying me. But that's for the two of us to work out. I don't want any of you putting any pressure on her about it, or bugging her about it, or anything else."

"Does she know you're telling us?" Emily asked.

Justin nodded. "She knows. Her parents know about it, and her cousins, but that's about it, I think. I would just as soon we all leave the spreading of the news up to her."

It was quiet for another moment as everyone stared at Justin. Then Cherokee Rose Chisholm let out a war whoop that any old-time Cherokee would have been proud of.

"Justin's going to be a father! We're having a baby!"

The room erupted in cheers and laughter and congratulations.

Later that night, lying in his lonely bed and wishing Blaire was there beside him, Justin called her number to tell her about his family's reaction to their news. The phone rang several times. Just when he thought she wouldn't answer, she did.

"Did I wake you?" he asked.

At the sound of his voice Blaire sniffed. "No. No, I'm awake."

"What's wrong?" he asked. "You sound funny."

She sniffed again. "Nothing's wrong. I've just been crying, that's all."

"Why?" he demanded. "What's happened? What's wrong? I can be there in twenty minutes."

"Only if you break every speed law in the county." Her mood lightened considerably. "But thank you for the thought. Nothing's wrong. It's just a hormone thing."

"Nothing's wrong?"

"Nothing new, anyway. Nothing that made me start crying, except these crazy hormones."

"Damn, honey, does this happen often?"

"Often enough," she said, relieved to have this latest crying jag behind her. "Did you tell your family?"

"I did. Tonight after supper. I called a family meeting, so Caleb and Mel were here for the news."

"Dare I ask?"

"How they took it? Oh, you know, lots of cheering and patting me on the back and asking how you're feeling and when the baby's due."

"Oh." Dammit, here came the tears again. There was nothing she could do to stop them. She hadn't been prepared for such acceptance from Justin's family.

Of course, she thought, sniffing back her suddenly drying tears, their reaction had probably been for his benefit, because they loved him. How they would act toward her, particularly if Justin wasn't around, might be an entirely different story.

"That's sweet," she added. "I'm glad they took the news so well."

"Are you kidding? They're ecstatic," he said.

Hesitantly, she asked, because she couldn't help herself. "What did they say about us not getting married?"

He was quiet for a moment, then said, "I won't lie to you. They're disappointed. But they promised not to interfere, or pressure you."

Well, she thought, that was something, at least. However, all she had to do was see one of his family and she would feel pressured. But there was nothing anyone could do about that.

"Blaire?"

"Oh, sorry. My mind wandered. I'm glad they're taking all this so well."

"Of course they are. We're talking about the next generation of Chisholms. A new cousin for Sloan's girls."

"You mean his new stepdaughters?"

"Step, according to Sloan, is only a word. He believes it's what's in the heart, not the DNA, that makes a family. Those are his girls, and there's no two ways about it."

"Your brother," Blaire said in awe, "is a very special man."

"He's not as special as I am," Justin claimed.

She smiled. "If you say so."

"I do, and don't you forget it. So, I'll bet your folks were glad to see you."

Blaire groaned. "Come on, Chisholm, we were having a nice, pleasant conversation here. Don't ruin it now."

"Trouble?"

"Nothing new," she said. "Just more of the same, and no, I don't want to talk about it."

"Are they after you to marry me?"

"I said I don't—"

"Was that a yes, or a no?" he asked.

"It was neither. It was, it's late and I've got an early day tomorrow."

"Yeah," he agreed. "So do I. My horse probably forgot what I look like, I've been gone so long."

"If you'd stayed home instead of following me all over the state, you wouldn't have that worry."

"If I hadn't trailed you nearly to Kansas, you'd still be sitting out there in that ditch in that little red tin can you call a car."

"I did thank you for rescuing me."

"Yes," he said, his voice turning deliberately suggestive. "You certainly did."

"Good night, Justin."

"Good night, Blaire. Say good-night to my kid for me."

Blaire hung up the phone and pressed a hand over her womb, feeling tears well up in her eyes again. "Oh, baby, what am I supposed to do about this daddy of yours? And what am I going to do about your Chisholm uncles and aunts and your great grandmother?"

It was the latter, Cherokee Rose Chisholm, who worried Blaire the most. The seventy-eight-year-old woman was a legend in the state of Oklahoma and beyond. She was known not only for her top-notch cattle and horses, but for her honesty, her generosity, and her loyalty, yet it was no secret that the lady didn't take any crap from anybody. How did she really feel about this new Chisholm not being raised in the Chisholm family?

Blaire got her chance to find out the next morning. At around ten o'clock a shiny silver SUV pulled up in the parking lot. The way the sun reflected off it, there was no way Blaire could miss it, sitting as she was, before the front window in her makeshift office in her parents' house.

The matriarch of the Chisholm clan stepped out of her vehicle as regally as any queen from her carriage. She even had a crown of sorts: her long black and iron-gray hair had been braided and the braid wrapped around her head. Her blue jeans were clean and crisp, her Western shirt piped in red and tucked into the waistband of her jeans, cinched by a brown leather belt with a big oval silver buckle. Her boots were hand-tooled and shined to within an inch of their lives.

In a deliberate, moderate stride, she crossed the parking lot and entered the feed store.

Sometime during the next few minutes Blaire realized that her fingernails were digging gouges into her palms. She purposely relaxed her hands, but a few seconds later realized they were knotted into fists again as she stared anxiously out the front window.

What was Rose Chisholm doing in there? What would she say to her father about the baby? What would her father say in return?

Blaire winced at the thought of the latter. He would have plenty to say, and all of it blaming Justin. Blaire would have to set the record straight as soon as she found out how much damage her father was doing to the Harding-Chisholm family relations.

A few minutes later Mrs. Chisholm came out of the store with a flat of yellow pansies.

Justin's favorite flower, Blaire noted. But she, herself, would have chosen purple, his favorite color, were she planting flowers for him.

Of course, Mrs. Chisholm was undoubtedly not planting to please her youngest grandson. More likely she planted to please herself.

The woman stashed the flowers in the back of her SUV then headed across the lot toward the house.

Blaire swallowed. There was no place to run, no place to hide from Justin's grandmother. If there was a way to postpone this meeting, or avoid it altogether, Blaire would do it. She had seen Mrs. Chisholm dozens of times over the years, but they had never held a conversation, or even spoken to each other, as far as Blaire could recall.

It looked as if that was all about to change.

At the sound of the doorbell Blaire jerked from the window. All right. She squared her shoulders and wiped her sweating palms down the thighs of her jeans. It was time to meet her child's great grandmother.

With her breath locked somewhere near the bottom of her lungs, Blaire made her way down the hall, into the living room, and to the front door. She opened the door and blinked. Up close, Rose Chisholm was even more striking. Her bronze skin was smooth and amazingly free of wrinkles, giving her a youthful appearance. Her deep brown eyes, which could have been hard or cold, smiled at her.

"Hello, Blaire." Mrs. Chisholm held out her hand. "I'm Rose."

Blaire let out her breath and accepted the handshake. "Of course. Come in, please."

"I suppose I should," she said, stepping in when Blaire moved aside. "Since I used checking on our account as an excuse to get your father to tell me where you were."

"If you really want to talk about your account, we can go to my office, otherwise, the living room is much more comfortable."

"Then let's be comfortable," Rose suggested with a smile. "Besides, since Sloan got smart and married Emily, she handles most of our bookkeeping now. The girl is a godsend. For several reasons, bookkeeping being only one of them."

Blaire led Rose to the sofa and motioned for her

to be seated. "Can I get you something to drink? My mother makes a fresh pitcher of iced tea every morning."

"No, thank you, my dear. I won't stay long. I just wanted to come by and let you know that Justin told us last night about the baby."

Blaire sank to the cushion beside Rose. "Yes. He called and told me."

Rose peered at her closely. "He said you knew he was telling us. Is that right?"

"Yes." Her lips twitched. "He asked my permission to tell you."

Rose nodded. "That's my Justin. I'm glad he hasn't forgotten his manners."

"Oh, no." This time Blaire smiled easily. "Justin is nothing if not polite."

Rose nodded again. "I'm glad to hear it. You'll pardon me for sticking my nose in, but I'm an old woman, with no guarantees of another year."

Blaire gasped and pressed a hand to Rose's forearm. "You're not ill, are you?"

"What? Oh, no. How sweet of you to ask. No, I just meant that I've already lived most of my life, so I don't like to dillydally around with what little time I've got left. Which is why I'm going to ask—did Justin ask you to marry him?"

Blaire felt heat sting her cheeks. She found she could not hold the woman's gaze. "Yes, he did. More than once. Please don't blame him for the two of us not getting married. It's my fault. I have my reasons for turning him down."

"And I won't ask what they are. I'll leave you that much privacy, at least," Rose added with a slight smile. "But don't be surprised if Justin tries to change your mind."

"No," Blaire said. "I won't."

"Is there anything you need?" Rose asked. "You or the baby? Whether you marry Justin or not, the child you carry makes you part of our family, and we take care of our own. We want to help in any way we can."

Blaire heard the sincerity in Rose's words, in her voice, and was humbled by it. "Thank you. All I really need right now is to get my car out of the shop, but it's not fixed yet, so no one can help with that."

"You're feeling well?" Rose asked. "You look as if you do."

"I'm fine, truly."

"Any morning sickness?"

Blaire rolled her eyes. "Yes. I'm afraid I gave Justin a demonstration of it yesterday morning."

Rose smiled widely. "Good for you. I always said women should share more of the joy of pregnancy and childbirth with their men."

Chapter Eleven

How ironic, Blaire thought that evening, that the only person who accepted her right to make her own decision about marriage was the grandmother of the very man Blaire refused to marry.

Oh, to have such acceptance from her own parents!

But that, Blaire knew, was too much to hope for.

Rose had stayed only a few minutes, but in those few minutes Blaire felt as if she'd found a true friend. Someone she could confide in, perhaps, who would not judge her.

Blaire wasn't fool enough to believe that Rose Chisholm would befriend anyone who hurt one of her own, though, so this tentative friendship could be temporary, indeed, if Blaire and Justin couldn't come to an amicable agreement regarding the baby. But Blaire felt they could. Hoped, prayed they could.

The dust had yet to settle from Rose's departure from the parking lot when Blaire's father flew out the back door of the store and marched across to the house.

"Well?" he demanded. "What did she want? Is she going to make that boy marry you?"

"Daddy!" Blaire stared at her father in shock. "You know perfectly well that Justin has asked to marry me, several times. I've told you that myself."

"Then why aren't you married, little girl?"

"Because," she said tightly, "I said no. No more!" She held her hand up to stop whatever he'd been about to say. "I'm not going to talk about it. Rose Chisholm trusts me to make the right decision. You're going to have to trust me, too."

Without waiting for her father to remark, Blaire spun on her heel and left the house. "I'm taking an early lunch." She dashed across the driveway to the garage and climbed the stairs to her apartment. There she slammed the door and locked herself in. And the world out.

What she wanted most in that moment, she realized, was Justin. And that realization appalled her. She had always winced in embarrassment whenever one of her girlfriends felt like running to a man so he could take care of things for her. Even her own mother was prone to expecting her husband to solve her problems for her.

Blaire refused to become that kind of woman, dependent upon a man to get through the day.

Good grief, she'd had an argument with her father and she wanted to run to Justin and cry on his shoulder? When had she turned into such a weak-kneed, lily-livered wimp?

On the other hand, she thought, what was wrong with a person wanting a little comfort, someone to take her side of things? The need for a little emotional support now and then didn't constitute a weakness. Did it?

To be on the safe side, when her phone rang that night, she did not answer.

No one left a message on her answering machine, and she didn't have caller ID, but she was sure it had been Justin. No one else would call her at ten o'clock at night.

The next night no one called. Neither did anyone call the night after that, nor the night after that. In fact, Blaire's phone did not ring for a solid week.

It was amazing, Justin thought, how much strength and energy and willpower it took not to make a phone call. Not to hop in his pickup and drive into town.

Not to grab his grandmother by the neck and shake her until she told him what went on at the feed store that day.

He must have it bad, not to be able to make it

through a single day without talking to Blaire, seeing her. Being near her.

All he'd managed to learn was that yes, Grandmother had gone to the feed store, and yes, she had spoken with Blaire. Blaire was a nice girl and it seemed as if she had a good head on her shoulders.

As for anything else that might have been discussed between the two most important women in his life, Cherokee Rose Chisholm's lips were apparently sealed. With superglue. The woman was flat not talking.

That, Justin could probably have lived with. But that new twinkle that had been in his grandmother's eyes since her return from town was driving him crazy.

"I will say one thing," his grandmother told him as she stopped before her bedroom door on her way to retire for the night. "That young woman needs a break. She's under a great deal of pressure from her parents, you, even herself. Everyone, including you, needs to back off for a few days and give her a chance to breathe, a chance to think for herself instead of being told what she should or shouldn't do."

"You think I'm pushing too hard?" he asked, already knowing the answer.

"If you aren't, I know you would like to."

Justin chuckled and kissed his grandmother's cheek. "You know me too well. I'll give her some time and space, but I'm not about to let her get away from me."

"No." She kissed his cheek in return. "I never thought you would."

He watched her enter her room and close the door, then he closed himself into his own bedroom. He would do his best to keep his word to his grandmother, for Blaire's sake, because he knew his grandmother was right.

But he couldn't just not call. He'd left her with the impression that she would hear from him today. One call, that would be all, and then he would back off for a while.

She didn't answer. He let it ring and ring and ring, and she didn't answer.

Maybe she was ready for that breather now instead of later.

A man who couldn't take a hint was at best a nuisance. At worst, a creep. All things considered, he would just as soon the mother of his child not think of him as a creep.

But as one day turned into another he began to wonder if maybe he really was in love with her. Why else would he feel this need to be with her, to hear her voice? Why else would he feel this constant yearning?

How was a man to know?

After three days of not calling her and not going to town, he still didn't know if he was in love, but everyone else came to believe he'd lost his marbles. He rode his horse out to the middle pasture, but came back without the calf he'd gone out there to get.

At supper that night six-year-old Janie was confused. "How come Daddy said Uncle Justin was out to lunch? It's suppertime, and he's not out, he's right here."

Her big sister, older by two years, rolled her eyes in disgust. "It's an expression, silly."

"Libby," Emily cautioned her daughter. "No name calling."

"Yes, ma'am."

"Well, what's it mean?" Janie demanded.

"It means," Libby said in her my-sister-is-an-im-becile tone, "that he's cuckoo."

"Oh." Janie slurped up another strand of spaghetti between pursed lips. "You mean like this afternoon when he tried to use the paintbrush to fix the flat tire on his pickup?"

"Yeah," Libby said. "Like that."

Justin made a face. "Didn't anybody ever tell you two it's not polite to talk about people when they're sitting right here?"

"Well, golly." Janie's little eyebrows lowered. "If you can't talk about people when they're right here, and you're not supposed to talk about 'em behind their backs, when can you talk about them?"

Emily cleared her throat to get the attention of her daughters. "I believe the lesson there is that it's not polite to talk about other people at all."

Libby's eyebrows climbed up her forehead. "If we can't talk about people, what are we gonna talk about?"

There was the unmistakable sound of muffled and

choked laughter as Sloan picked up the large bowl of mashed potatoes and started it around the table.

A full week after Justin had brought Blaire home from Stillwater, he finally gave in and drove to town. If asked, he would swear that his pickup turned off Main into the parking lot of the feed store all on its own. Surely he himself had more willpower than to play the lovesick high school teen and drive by his girl's house.

Hell, he thought. At least he hadn't driven by and honked.

Of course he hadn't. He'd parked and gotten out, walked into her father's store without proper mental preparation. And Tom Harding was waiting for him with both barrels, metaphorically speaking.

"Why haven't you married my girl yet?" Harding demanded.

Justin glanced around to find himself the only customer inside. The others, who belonged to the other vehicles in the lot, must have been out in the warehouse. It was a common place to run into friends and hang around for a visit.

"Well?" Harding barked.

How was he supposed to answer? The simple truth was, he would marry Blaire in a heartbeat, had asked her several times, but she had turned him down. If he said as much to her father the man was likely to take it out on her in some way.

In the end, Justin shrugged. "That's something Blaire and I will have to work out between the two of us."

"Well, get to working it out, before the kid graduates high school."

"Thanks for the advice." Having completely forgotten the excuse he had used to come to the store, Justin turned and left.

Outside, he stepped off the porch-cum-loading dock and drew to a halt. Beyond his left shoulder stood the Hardings' house, where Blaire was probably working at that very moment. Straight ahead sat his pickup.

To the left, possible—probably—humiliation, because he wouldn't be able to stop himself from asking her yet again to marry him, and she would once again turn him down.

Straight ahead, escape.

From the window in her office, the same window from which she had watched Rose Chisholm arrive nearly a week ago, Blaire saw Justin standing in the parking lot.

She'd seen him arrive about ten minutes earlier, had still been at the window when he left the store. Now he simply stood there, as if trying to decide what to do.

Blaire smoothed her hair and unrolled the sleeves of her shirt. Her makeup could use a little refreshing, but she didn't have time. He would be knocking on the door any second.

This is, if he ever decided to move, she thought with a frown. What was he doing just standing there? Oh, he looked good. The weather was mild enough that he wore a flannel shirt with no jacket or overcoat. The breeze was strong enough to ruffle his hair back from his face and redden his cheeks.

She had missed him. She could admit that to herself, privately. She had missed his face, his phone calls, his laughter.

Why was he just standing there? Why wasn't he coming to the house to see her?

Whatever she'd eaten for lunch—and for the life of her, she couldn't remember what it was even though she'd eaten it less than an hour ago—must not be agreeing with her, because she felt a burning ache beneath her ribs. It had come on sharply the instant she'd realized Justin was not coming to see her.

This was…well, it was wrong, that's what it was. He wasn't supposed to ignore her, and if he did, she certainly wasn't supposed to ache because of it.

The man was turning her life upside down, making her want him, giving her a child, expecting her to marry him, sending his grandmother to see her. Then, ignoring her?

No, this wasn't right. Tugging on her cardigan sweater, Blaire marched out of the house and across the parking lot. She was twenty feet away from Justin when he turned and took a step toward her. Only then, after he'd turned and moved in her direction, did he seem to notice her.

"Blaire."

She stopped about five feet away. "Justin."

"Hi." He stuck his hands in his hip pockets. "How are you doing?"

"Just fine." Not that he'd bothered to call and find out all week long, she thought with an odd mixture of pain and anger and sadness. And maybe just a touch of peevishness, but that was neither here nor there. Then she went and ruined her aloof act. "I thought maybe you would have called this past week."

He dragged his boot heel through the gravel beneath his feet. "I wanted to."

She wasn't going to ask. It would sound too pitiful, too needy. She wouldn't give him that much of an edge over her. Then she did. "Why didn't you?"

He glanced out at the cars going past on Main. "You asked me for breathing room. I said I'd give it to you." He nodded toward her compact parked beside the garage. "I see you got your car back. I thought you were going to call me for a ride back to Stillwater to get it."

"They called yesterday. Mama took me."

"Oh." He stared down at his feet, then glanced back up at her. "Did they fix everything?"

"It looks fine. Now all it needs is painting, but I'm in no hurry for that."

"I can—"

"No, you can't," she told him. "But thank you for offering. I got a cell phone yesterday."

"That's…" It did her heart good to see him look both relieved and disappointed. She knew he'd wanted to get it for her himself. "…great."

"Have you got something to write with? I'll give you the number," she offered.

He had a small notebook not much larger than a business card, and a short pencil stub in his shirt pocket. She gave him the number of her new cell phone and he wrote it in his notebook.

They stood there another few minutes, looking everywhere but at each other.

"Justin, what's wrong?" she finally asked.

"What do you mean?"

"I mean you're acting like we're strangers or something. Are you angry with me?"

"Why should I be angry with you?"

She shrugged and hugged her arms around her middle. "Because I won't marry you?"

"Ah," he said with a slight smile. "There's where you're wrong."

"Wrong?"

"I think you will marry me. You just haven't realized that's what you want to do yet."

"Ah," she mimicked. "There's that ego we all know and love. I'd wondered what had happened to it."

He chuckled. "Just like a woman. Give her what

she says she wants and she wonders what's wrong. Have lunch with me tomorrow. Maybe we can regain our footing with each other."

"All right." She didn't even have to think about her answer. Not with the way her heart lifted at his invitation.

For their lunch date the next day, the weather decided to be their friend. The temperature soared to sixty, the air barely stirred, and the sun shone true and bright. A two-shirt day at the most.

Blaire dressed in jeans, shirt, boots, and an oversized red flannel shirt as a jacket.

To Justin, when he pulled up and she stepped out of her apartment and started down the stairs toward him, she looked adorable. But then, she always looked adorable to him.

He rounded his rig and opened the passenger door for her. Before he could offer her a hand up, she climbed in unaided.

Okay, he thought with reluctance. She's not ready to be touched yet. That was a shame, because he certainly was, as long as the person doing the touching was her.

All of this obsessing he'd been doing lately, thinking of her, dreaming of her, wanting her. It had to mean something, didn't it?

"Where are we going?" she asked when he jumped into the driver's seat and pulled out of the parking lot.

"It's a surprise." And a gamble, he thought. A gamble for him.

"Oh? Okay." But her agreeable tone turned wary a moment later when he took the road out of town. "Justin?"

"Hmm?"

"You did say we were going to lunch, didn't you?"

"I did, and we are. Just trust me. You'll like it." He hoped.

He stayed on the highway for several miles, then turned off onto a secondary road before reaching the main gate to the Cherokee Rose Ranch. He followed the secondary road for a mile and turned to drive along the back side of the ranch until he reached his favorite spot.

He pulled off onto the narrow shoulder and parked.

By this time Blaire had her arms crossed over her chest as if to protect herself, but she was looking around with interest.

"I thought you might enjoy a picnic, since it's so nice today," he said.

She studied the landscape outside her window. "This is the place you told me about, isn't it."

"Yeah," he confessed, wondering what she thought of it. "Yeah, it is."

She opened her door and got out. She walked over to the barbed-wire fence and looked around. Justin got out and followed her. The land sloped gently up from the fence to crest about fifty yards away from where they stood. The Bermuda grass was winter brown now, but in the summer it would be a thick green carpet, broken here and there by the occasional scrub oak.

"I guess I don't know what a persimmon tree looks like," Blaire confessed. "Or a buffalo wallow, either, for that matter."

He couldn't say how pleased he was that she had remembered his description of the place. "Come on, I'll show you." He crawled through the fence, then pushed one strand down with his boot and held the one above it up with both hands while Blaire climbed carefully through.

Then, because he had opportunity and a good excuse, he took her hand in his as he led her toward the small grove of tall, rather narrow trees at the far end of the clearing with scarcely a leaf left on them anywhere.

"These," he said with a wave of his free hand, "are persimmon trees. Although, I can't prove it because the deer picked them clean months ago."

"It's just as well," she said. "But I'm wondering if a ripe persimmon is as awful as a green one."

"Ripe ones are sweet," he told her. "You can try one out next fall."

He could have kicked himself for referring to the future that way, when they might not have a future together at all. But she didn't protest, and she had yet to pull her hand from his, so he held on and led her up the slight incline to the crest and over.

"Have you ever seen a buffalo wallow before?" he asked her.

"Not that I know of," she answered. "If I have I didn't know what it was."

He stopped at the lip of a ragged depression in the ground, perhaps two feet deep at its deepest in the center. "It looks pretty much like that."

"That? That looks like erosion."

"I guess that's what it is. Erosion caused by years of big heavy animals rolling around on their backs in the same spot. They wear it down, the rain comes along and helps things along a little more, and there you have it."

She cocked her head and studied the wallow. "Has anyone ever tried to fill one in?"

Justin shrugged. "I'm sure they have. We haven't. Haven't had a need to." He stepped off the edge, taking Blaire with him, and walked inside the ten-foot-wide depression. "The ground in here is so hard-packed not much will grow. Besides," he said looking around at the pasture. "With all the buffalo gone—most of them, anyway—I kinda like leaving this here, a reminder of the huge herds that used to roam here."

"It's good," she said. "That you want to preserve it."

Justin had never cared much one way or another whether people outside his family approved of him or not, but the approval Blaire had just given him made his chest swell.

Still holding her hand, he led her up and out of the wallow and back along the crest to the center of the hilltop.

"Here," he told her, "is where I want to build a house."

"The view would be spectacular," she observed.

"It will." He looked out over the countryside and imagined seeing it from his very own porch. With Blaire at his side. And a child at their feet.

The picture in his mind of the three of them on their porch was so powerful it nearly brought him to his knees. He knew, in that instant, that his life, the home he hoped for, his entire future would be sadly lacking without Blaire. He was in love with her.

Why hadn't he seen it sooner? Why hadn't he understood his own feelings?

Now what did he do? Blurt it out? *By the way, Blaire, I was wrong. I really do love you.*

Sure, she would believe that. What woman wouldn't?

He could give her flowers, but he didn't have any. This time of year he couldn't even come up with any wildflowers. The only flowers he'd seen lately were the yellow pansies his grandmother had planted a few days ago. He doubted she would approve of his picking them, and Blaire might not appreciate stolen flowers anyway.

"Justin?"

He pulled himself out of his musings to realize that he'd been crushing her fingers. "Damn. I'm sorry. Did I hurt you?"

"I'm fine," she assured him. "Is something wrong?"

"Wrong? No, of course not. What could be wrong?"

Blaire didn't know, but something was going on. She felt a sudden new tension in and around him.

"I think I promised you lunch," he said.

"I think you're right. You did."

"Then lunch it is. I'll be right back."

"Back?" she protested as he started down the slope toward the road. "You're leaving me here?"

"I'm just going to the pickup," he called back to her.

Blaire watched as he sprinted the last few yards. She flexed her fingers, then folded them against her palm, still feeling the warmth of his hand against hers. Still wondering what had gone through his mind a moment ago when his face had gone blank and his fingers had squeezed hers.

In a way, it was gratifying to realize that something bothered him. He always seemed so sure of himself and positive about what he wanted. He'd brought her here to show her where he planned to build his home one day.

His home. Not theirs. This had been his plan for a long time and had nothing to do with her or the baby.

Why that should disappoint her, she didn't know. What a stupid thing for her to feel, particularly when she'd been pushing him away for weeks.

Look at him, she thought. He even walks like a man who knows exactly what he wants.

He climbed through the fence and circled around to the driver's side of the pickup. From behind the seat he pulled what looked to be an old quilt. From the bed he retrieved an ice chest and a gallon sized Thermos.

Blaire met him at the fence and took the quilt and jug so he could use both hands to carry the large ice chest.

After climbing through the fence for the third time that day, Justin eyed it critically. "Need a gate here," he muttered.

They carried their load up the slope and Justin picked a spot that he hoped would one day be the center of his front yard. There he spread out the quilt.

"Lunch," he said, placing the ice chest on one corner of the quilt, "is served, m'lady."

"Why, thank you, kind sir." She dropped to her knees before the ice chest and opened the top. "What are we having?"

They were having fried chicken, potato salad, coleslaw, fruit salad, and for dessert, fresh, homemade brownies, with iced tea to wash it down.

"If you tell me you cooked all of this yourself," she told him as she licked chocolate from her fingers, "I might change my mind and marry you after all."

She meant it as a joke, but he didn't laugh. The best he had to offer was a half-smile.

"I can't even take credit for the ice cubes. We have an ice maker. But I'll give you a better reason. Last week when you asked me if I loved you I said I didn't know. Now I know. I do love you, Blaire."

Blaire's heart started pounding against her ribs.

"I love you and want to spend the rest of my life with you," he said. "I want us to build a home here on this hill, but if you'd rather live in town, I can go along with that. As long as you marry me, because I really do love you."

Blaire's hands were shaking, and so was her head. "You don't mean that."

"Of course I mean it," he claimed.

"No." She shook her head harder and scooted away from him. She couldn't let herself believe him. "No one else in my life has ever loved me. I'm supposed to believe you just because you say so?"

"How can I prove it to you?" he asked.

"You can't. You could take out a sign with two-foot letters and I wouldn't believe it. All you want to do is control me."

"Dammit, Blaire, I'm not your father, and you're not your mother."

"'Get a cell phone,'" she mimicked. "I got one. 'Get a safer car.' I didn't. I like my car just fine. 'Stay out of the cold.' Ha. You like telling me what to do. I don't like being told."

"I don't want to control your life, dammit, I want to share it. I love you. I want us to become a family. You, me and the baby."

But Blaire was not hearing him. Her fear had turned his words into a buzzing in her ears.

Chapter Twelve

Blaire scarcely remembered the ride home from her picnic with Justin at the Cherokee Rose, and that was more to her shame than her credit.

For one brief second, when he'd first told her he loved her, Blaire had allowed herself to believe.

Then a sharp picture of her parents had intruded, and reality came crashing in around her head. She could not afford to believe. She couldn't let herself be rushed or pressured into marriage. No matter what he said, it was all still because of the baby, and that was no reason for them to tie themselves to each other.

As if to prove her correct, that night her parents lit into each other again, over nothing, as far as Blaire could tell. But their argument ended with the usual accusations of whose fault it was that they were stuck with each other.

No, Blaire would not believe Justin. She would not marry him. She would not live her life the way her parents did, and she would not expose her child to such bitterness as theirs. If that left her feeling sad and lonely, as if she might be making the biggest mistake of her life…. No. She couldn't afford to think like that.

All she had to do now was make Justin believe that she would not change her mind, that he should give up on her and get on with his life. They would work something out regarding the baby, because she had meant it when she'd said she didn't intend to cut him out of the child's life. Her child would know its father. She would make sure of that. But her child would never be made to feel responsible for its parents' problems. Not as long as Blaire had breath in her body.

Justin was not as lucky as Blaire. He remembered every second of the rest of their time together that afternoon. The painful, echoing silence. The terror and anger emanating from her.

He thought he understood the terror, although the strength of it surprised and worried him. But the anger was new and, to him, inexplicable.

She had told him she would not marry a man who didn't love her. Now he loved her, and her reaction was anger? It didn't make sense.

Maybe it was time for him to face the fact that she didn't return his feelings. She most especially didn't share his desire for marriage.

What if he got lucky and was finally able to convince her to marry him? It seemed to him that they ran the risk of making her feel trapped somewhere down the road. Did he want to marry a woman who needed her arm twisted, so to speak? Would she one day turn into her mother and throw it back in his face that getting married had never been her idea?

God help him, he was going crazy. Was it time to push harder, or let go?

Let go, hell. He didn't think he was capable of that. He was nowhere near ready to give in. Which was why, two days after their picnic, he called her and asked her to lunch.

"Indoors, this time," he added quickly. "With a waitress and everything. No barbed-wire fences, no buffalo wallows."

"Oh, I don't know," she told him. "I didn't mind the fence, and I liked the buffalo wallow."

"You did?"

"I did. But as for lunch—"

"Tomorrow, around noon?" he asked.

"I can't, Justin."

"How about the day after?"

"No, thank you. I'm sorry. I have to go."

Justin was left listening to a dial tone.

On the other end of the line, Blaire dropped the

phone into its cradle. Her hands shook so hard she couldn't have held the receiver another ten seconds if her life had depended on it.

She had blown it. Justin had presented her with the perfect opportunity to tell him not to ask her out again, not to call her any more. But she had panicked and hung up.

The next time, she promised herself. If he asked her out again, she would be firm and honest and explain that she was never going to change her mind.

But when he pulled into the parking lot two days later, her first instinct was to run so she wouldn't have to face him.

"When did I get to be such a total coward?" she wondered aloud.

"Did you say something, honey?"

Blaire slapped a hand over her heart to keep it from leaping from her chest. "Mama! I didn't know you were there."

"Sorry." Nancy Harding laughed. Then she glanced out the window of Blaire's office and her eyes widened. "Oh, look! There's Justin."

"Yes." Blaire swallowed around the knot of nerves that rose in her throat. There was no way she could talk to Justin with her mother hanging on every word. "I was just going out to say hi. I'll be back in a few minutes."

"Oh, but don't you want to invite him in? I've got a full pitcher of tea, but I could make coffee if he'd prefer that."

"Never mind the tea and coffee." Blaire brushed past her mother and headed for the front door. "I doubt he'll be staying." In fact, it would be Blaire's mission to see that he didn't want to stay. That he didn't want to return, or call or anything else.

She squared her shoulders, screwed up her courage, and marched out to the parking lot, where she met him before he'd made it five feet from his pickup.

"Hi." He smiled and pulled off the cowboy hat he'd been wearing.

"Hi." She resisted the urge to wipe her sweaty palms on her jeans. "Justin, I—"

"Sunday after church the whole family eats at Lucille's," he told her. "I was hoping you'd join us this Sunday. It's public, so you'd be able to get up and leave any time you wanted. I thought that might make your first meal with the whole clan a little less stressful."

"Justin, this isn't going to work."

"What isn't going to work?"

"None of it," she said earnestly. "You and me. We're not going to work."

He stared at her so long that she shifted her weight several times from one foot to the other.

"We're not?" he asked.

"No." She swallowed again. "I'm sorry. But I can't marry you, and I won't change my mind."

He moved a step closer to her. "You don't care that I'm in love with you? It means nothing?"

"It might, but I don't think you do love me, Justin, and I don't trust myself enough to be able to tell. I can't risk it."

"You can't risk it? This is our lives we're talking about. Our child's life. Life doesn't come with guarantees."

"I know that," she cried. "I'm not asking you for one. I just have to feel it, down deep inside. Feel that I can trust myself, trust you, and I don't feel that. To be honest, I think I'm too scared to feel it."

"Scared of what? Of me?" he cried, incredulous. "You think I would ever knowingly hurt you? I couldn't, Blaire. I simply couldn't. I *love* you."

She shook her head hard and backed away from him. "Justin, please."

"Please what? Please don't love you?"

"Don't push me. The harder you push, the more I want to resist."

"I've noticed," he said harshly. "I supposed now you're going to run."

"Run?"

"That's what you do, isn't it? When things get uncomfortable. Which cousin will you go see this time?"

The fact that she had been contemplating doing just as he accused sent heat rushing to her cheeks.

"Aha!" He pointed a finger at her face. "I'm right, aren't I? It's right there on your face."

"Don't be ridiculous. If I want to go visit my cousins, I'll go, and you don't have anything to say about it. Go home, Justin, and don't call me anymore. The baby's not due until September. I'll let you know when it comes."

"September?" His eyebrows rose at least an inch, his voice at least an octave. "If you think for one minute I'm going to stand back and not involve myself in your life until after the baby is born, you've got another think coming."

Blaire closed her eyes and tried to pull her hair out with both hands at her temples. "I didn't mean that we wouldn't have any contact. I didn't mean it like that. You make me crazy. I won't go out with you, I won't date you, I won't spend the night with you. I won't marry you. I will talk with you, about the baby, but I don't want you calling me every day, or even every week."

"Sometimes, sweetheart, we don't always get what we want."

Blaire would have demanded to know what he meant by that, but for a moment she was too astounded by his words to speak. By the time she found her voice and her wits, he was back in his pickup and pulling out into the street.

By the time Justin got home he had a red mark on the outer edge of his hand from pounding his fist against the steering wheel in frustration.

How could he have been so stupid as to push her the way he had? And that stupid parting comment of his—*Sometimes, sweetheart, we don't always get what we want.* Where the hell had that come from?

But he knew the answer there. It had come from his gut. She said she didn't want him. For one knife-edged moment, he had believed her, and that knife-edge had sliced deep.

Then he'd seen the lie in her eyes. It wasn't that she didn't want him, it was that she was afraid to trust. Not him, but herself. She still had it in her head that the two of them would end up bickering for the next thirty years the way her parents did.

Justin shuddered at the thought. It couldn't happen, because he wasn't a man to bicker. He had never played the blame game, or griped about his problems. He was more into practical jokes and tending his cattle and horses.

But Blaire didn't know that about him. She didn't know much of anything about him, he realized. How could he expect her to simply take his word that things would work out between them?

Before that would happen, she had to believe that he truly loved her.

You could take out a sign with two-foot letters and I wouldn't believe it.

"Blaire Harding, you're gonna eat those words."

In less than an hour, Justin had a full-fledged plan for convincing Blaire that his feelings were true. But he wouldn't be able to do it alone. He enlisted both of his brothers and his two sisters-in-law. His grandmother agreed to take care of Janie and Libby for the night.

On the Internet he found the company he needed, located in Oklahoma City. He called in a rush order, then drove to the city to pick it up. When he got home late that night, that's when he would need his brothers and their wives.

It was going to be a long night.

His entire future rested on the outcome.

He was scared spitless that it wouldn't work, but he'd be damned if he could think of anything else to do.

Blaire cried herself to sleep that night. If she had been uncertain before, there was no question left now in her mind or heart. She was in love with Justin Chisholm.

He said he was in love with her. Why couldn't she take him at his word and accept his proposal? Why did she have to think up all these damn problems that might not ever arise between them? Why did she work so hard to convince herself that he didn't really love her?

What did she think, that he was lying? Simply trying to get her to marry him so he could get his hands on their child?

What kind of sense did that make?

Sure, she knew family was the most important thing to a Chisholm, but would he really go to the trouble of lying to her and marrying her just to have a family of his own?

The only other alternative to support her theory that he didn't actually love her, if he wasn't outright lying, was that he didn't know his own mind and heart.

That was much more likely, to her mind. Both of his brothers had married in the past few months. He was wrapped up in the romance of weddings and babies and thought he was in love with her.

That wasn't enough for her. She would not take advantage of his kind heart and his sense of family. Those two things were not enough upon which to build a marriage.

She was going to prove him right, much to her shame. She was going to show her cowardice by leaving town, just as he had predicted. If not for the health insurance coverage she enjoyed by working for her father, she would leave town permanently. But she could not afford to lose her insurance with a baby on the way. She wasn't that big a fool.

When dawn came the next morning her eyes were red streaked, red rimmed and swollen. Her morning sickness attacked with a vengeance.

She was growing to hate that toilet. When she was good and done with morning sickness she was going to have it replaced. Maybe she'd get a pink one this time instead of the utilitarian white she'd been hugging every morning lately.

A new duffel bag—maybe even an actual suit-case—would soon be in order if she continued to travel so much. She was going to Gayle's in Stillwater this time. She had called her last night to make sure her cousin would be home and could accommodate her.

Telling her parents she was leaving had been difficult. Like climbing Mount Everest might be difficult.

Insurance or no insurance, Blaire had some serious thinking to do about how she was going to raise her child out from under the influence of her parents. She wanted them to be a part of her child's life, but not every day, and not in a way that gave them the idea that they had some sort of say over the baby. She had no intention of fighting that battle every day of her life, and knowing her mother, it would be a battle royal.

But first things first, and that meant getting out of town long enough to let her parents and Justin know that she meant business.

She was putting the last of her things into her duffel when her phone rang. Surprised, she glanced at the clock. It was barely 8:00 a.m. No one she knew would call that early, except family. Or maybe Justin, she thought with a frown.

She thought about letting her answering machine get it, but finally grabbed up the receiver. "Yes?"

"Blaire, is that you? It's Nadine. Nadine White."

"Nadine?" They'd been in the same class in high school. Nadine now ran a beauty shop on Main near the grocery store. "What's up?"

Nadine laughed. "That's what I want to know. Have you been outside yet this morning?"

"Outside? No, why?"

Nadine shrieked something into the phone that Blaire didn't quite make out.

"What? Did you say something about a banner?"

"On Main. Go! Get your butt out the door and down the street, girlfriend. You won't believe it! Or maybe you will, but it 'bout knocked my socks off."

"Nadine, what are you talking about?"

"I'm taking about the banner strung across Main Street. Get out there and have a look. Then call me back and tell me what the devil's going on that I've been missing out on."

Before Blaire could comment, Nadine had hung up. No sooner had Blaire replaced the receiver than the phone rang again. This time it was Blaire's mother.

"Bunny Gonzales just called."

"And?" Bunny Gonzales worked at the hardware store and had been her mother's best friend for years. A call from Bunny didn't usually cause the quiver of excitement Blaire heard in her mother's voice, nor did it require that Blaire's mother report to Blaire.

"Before you leave town," her mother said breathlessly, "you need to drive east down Main until you can see the water tower."

Blaire frowned. "Whatever for?"

"Just do it! And take your camera!"

"Mama, what are you talking about? I'm not going to drive around looking at the stupid water tower."

"You will if you know what's good for you. There's not a girl alive who won't be pea green with envy of you. Now you go look, and then you come back here and tell me what you think."

As with Nadine, the phone went dead in her ear.

What was the matter with everyone? Had they all gone crazy? What could they possibly be talking about?

Truly curious now, Blaire pulled on her coat, then grabbed her duffel and overnight case. There was no sense coming back upstairs just to get them after she'd seen the stupid water tower.

She was halfway down the outside stairs when she glanced at her car and noticed someone had stuck a piece of white paper beneath her windshield wiper.

It gave her a shiver to think that someone had been right there at the foot of her stairs during the night and she hadn't been aware of it.

For that matter, she thought, coming to an abrupt halt at the foot of the stairs, *someone* had done a whole lot more than put a piece of paper under her wiper blade. A row of signs, about two-foot square, each on a wooden stake about three feet tall, marched from the foot of her stairs, along the edge of the parking lot, clear out to the street.

There must have been...six. She counted six signs, all white with red lettering, all saying the same thing:

JUSTIN LOVES BLAIRE

Blaire's heart gave a little leap in her chest. Justin had done this? He had come to her apartment during the night and planted these signs like a teenager trying to impress his girl?

She slapped a hand over her mouth and blinked. *Oh, Justin.*

With knees trembling, she walked around her car and set her duffel and overnighter on the ground. Her fingers weren't as nimble as they should have been when she plucked the paper from beneath her wiper blade and unfolded it.

BLAIRE, I REALLY DO LOVE YOU. JUSTIN

She pressed the note to her lips and looked around frantically, wondering if he was there, somewhere close, watching her reaction to his outrageous deeds.

"Oh, my God, the banner! The water tower! He wouldn't!"

Scrambling in her purse for her keys, Blaire jumped into her car and tore out of the parking lot, completely forgetting the belongings she'd left sitting in the gravel.

"Justin," she muttered to herself, "what have you done? What are you doing, you crazy man?"

She was three blocks from the center of town when she saw the banner. Strung across the intersection three blocks ahead, it was three feet high and white, with giant purple letters.

JUSTIN LOVES BLAIRE

Blaire braked to a halt in the middle of the street and stared, her mouth hanging open. Someone drove by and honked, but she couldn't look away from the banner to see who it was.

What had she said to him that day of the picnic? *You could take out a sign with two-foot letters and I wouldn't believe it.*

"Oh, my God." Justin had done her one better. Those letters had to be taller than two feet.

"The water tower!" Oh, good heavens! She stomped on the gas pedal and ran the red light without a care. There were sometimes more important things than obeying traffic laws, and this was one of those times. Besides, she looked first and there were no cars coming from either direction. This was Rose Rock, after all, not the big city.

Neither the water tower nor Justin Chisholm let Blaire down. Way up there on the tank at the top of the town's only water tower, in three-foot purple letters painted over the silver tank:

BLAIRE, WILL YOU MARRY ME? JUSTIN

"Oh!" She sat in the middle of the side street that gave her the best view of the tower and felt tears stream down her cheeks. She couldn't stop them and didn't try. If ever there was a time for tears, this was it.

"Oh, Justin." How could she possibly think he wasn't really in love with her now? What was a woman to do with a man like him? She must have hurt him terribly yesterday when she'd essentially told him to get lost.

"Oh, Justin." From her purse she pulled out her new cell phone and called the Cherokee Rose Ranch. Emily, Sloan's wife, answered.

"This is Blaire Harding."

"Blaire! Hello. It's so good to hear from you. I've been meaning to get into town to visit you, but haven't been able to get away lately. How are you doing?"

"I'm doing fine. I'm looking for Justin. Is he around?"

"No, he's out and about somewhere. I notice his pickup is gone, so there's no telling where he is. Did you try his cell?"

Blaire felt like an idiot. He'd given her his cell number. She should have called it first. "No," she told Emily, "but I will. Thanks."

She didn't give Emily time to say anything. She had to find Justin.

But he wasn't answering his cell. She left him a message and asked him to call her back.

With nothing else to do but wait to hear from him, Blaire drove home, astounded to find her duffel and overnight case sitting in the gravel, where she'd left them. She parked her car and carried her bags back upstairs.

When a half hour went by and Justin hadn't called, she tried his cell number again. Still no answer. "Call me, Justin. Please?"

But another half hour went by and he didn't call.

Suddenly Blaire couldn't wait around any longer. She knew what she had to do.

She went outside and crossed to the warehouse. From there she loaded the items she needed into her trunk.

"If Justin calls or comes by," she called to her father in the warehouse, "tell him I've gone on a picnic."

"A what?" her father yelled back.

"A picnic!"

"Now?"

"Now," she called back. "Just tell him."

Blaire pulled up at the spot where Justin wanted to build a house and felt her chest tighten. He wasn't there. She'd been so sure, after she'd driven out of town, that this was where she would find him. That he would be waiting here for her to come and say she was sorry she hadn't believed him when he'd said he loved her.

Well, there was no sense sitting around feeling sorry for herself. He wanted to make her sweat, that was his right. She had turned him away how many times?

She tugged on an old pair of leather work gloves, popped open her trunk, and got to work.

It was midmorning before Justin worked up the nerve to listen to the voice mail on his cell phone.

No relief there. "Call me." What the hell did that mean? Did it mean she believed him now? Or did it mean she was going to take out a restraining order against him if he went near her again?

Her second message wasn't much better, but at least on that one she'd said *please*.

There was no help for it. If he wanted to know how she was taking his little messages, he would have to go see her, face-to-face. If he could manage to avoid running into anyone he knew. He was going to take a serious ribbing for this, he knew. But if it won him Blaire, it would all be worth it.

But when he pulled in at the feed store, her car wasn't there. By God, if she'd left town without even seeing what he'd done—

Not possible. She would have seen the signs along her driveway and the note under her wiper blade. If she left town after that, the banner and the water tower wouldn't have mattered. Her leaving would mean she didn't care.

Gritting his teeth, he used his cell phone to return her call. When she answered, he asked, "Where are you?"

"Where am I? Where are you? I've been calling all over looking for you."

"And I'm calling you back, aren't I?"

"You took your own sweet time about it," she complained.

"Blaire, where are you?"

"I'm working on a landscaping project."

"Since when are you a landscaper? And what the hell do you plant in February?"

"Well," she said slowly, "since I'm planting it at your place, you should probably come see for yourself."

"My place? The house?"

"There's no house here yet, but I expect there will be before long."

Justin's heart gave a giant thud. "Don't move. You hear me, Blaire? Don't you move. I'm on my way."

He made the thirty-minute drive in twenty-two minutes. He found her on the other side of the fence, on her knees in the dirt. When he pulled over onto the shoulder and killed the engine, he was gratified by the way she darted through the fence and ran to greet him.

Perhaps, he thought as she neared, gratified was too tame a word. Overjoyed. Ecstatic. Grateful.

"Justin!"

He held out his arms and she ran into them as though she'd been waiting to do just that for her entire life. "Justin, I'm sorry I didn't believe you."

He took her by the shoulders and held her slightly away from him so he could see her face. "Do you believe me now?"

She gave him a smile that wobbled. "How can I not?"

"And what is it that you believe?"

Her lips pursed. "Is this a test?"

"I just want to make sure we're on the same page."

"I believe," she told him carefully, "that you love me. Maybe as much as I love you."

That stopped him. He'd thought she loved him, but she'd never said so. "You love me?"

"I love you."

"Then what are we going to do about it?" he asked.

"Well, first you should kiss me."

"I can do that." He kissed her, deeply and slowly, until they were both breathing hard. "Now what?"

"Now, we get married."

Justin tried to swallow past the sudden, huge knot of emotion in his throat and couldn't. "Married?" he managed.

"Married. If you're still willing."

With his knees turning weak, he leaned back against his pickup and pulled her with him. "I'm more than willing. How fast can we do it?"

Blaire threw her head back and laughed in sheer joy and relief. She hadn't ruined things with her fears. He still loved her, and she felt her love for him well up inside and fill her to the brim.

"We could elope," she said, "but our families would never forgive us."

"You're right. Two weeks?" he asked. "How does that sound?"

"It sounds like a lifetime," she told him. "But I doubt we can get it done any faster. Justin?"

He pulled her close and hugged her. "What is it?"

"Will you tell me again?"

"Tell you what?"

"You know."

"That I love you?" He peered down into her golden brown eyes.

She nodded. "I need to hear it again."

"You're going to hear it until you're sick of it, and then you're going to hear it some more. For the rest of our lives. I love you, Blaire. I love you."

"And I love you, Justin. Be my husband, help me raise our child. Help me raise purple pansies."

"What?" he frowned and blinked.

"Pansies." With a huge grin Blaire motioned toward the flowerbeds she had been planting with his favorite flowers. "Purple ones." His favorite color.

Justin swallowed around the huge lump in his throat. "I would be honored to marry you and raise babies—and flowers."

Epilogue

In the end it was three full weeks before they were able to stand before God and their families and exchange their vows.

The whole county was buzzing about how all three Chisholm men had taken the plunge in a matter of months.

The general consensus seemed to be that when those Chisholms fell, they fell hard and fast.

The Chisholms in question could find nothing in that statement to argue against.

During the three weeks that Blaire spent holding her mother back from putting on a huge production instead of the small ceremony Blaire and Justin wanted, Justin was not idle. He purchased—with

Blaire's approval—a three-bedroom mobile home and had it moved in near the persimmon grove. He'd purposely left the crest of the hill vacant, so the builders could get to work as soon as Blaire and Justin had picked out the plans for the house they wanted.

It also being calving season, Justin was kept more than busy. Since the calves didn't stop being born just because the youngest Chisholm got married, a honeymoon would have to wait. But Blaire was not disappointed by that. She moved into the mobile home and continued to work at the feed store, but only part-time.

The new house was finished in July, leaving plenty of time for Blaire to outfit the nursery before the baby came.

As summer drew to a close, Blaire, now covered under Justin's insurance plan, left the bookkeeping at the feed store once again to her mother, for good this time. Blaire had more than enough to do to put the final decorating touches on the house and get ready for the baby. And think about her new teaching job next year.

One of the local elementary teachers just found out she was expecting her first child. Come next February she planned to quit working. The school board offered the mid-year position to Blaire, who snapped it up.

Knowing how much she missed teaching, Justin fully supported her decision to go back to work next winter. By February they might have a handle on this baby business. Maybe.

The baby chose Labor Day weekend to put in an appearance. The entire Chisholm clan, plus Blaire's parents and cousins, were on hand for the blessed event.

Justin proudly played catch during the birth and got to make the announcement: "It's a boy!" If there were tears in his eyes, that was okay, as they went with the ones in his voice.

Blaire could barely tell through the sheen of her own tears.

They named him John, after Justin's grandfather, and Thomas, after his great-grandfather.

Upon learning that her first great-grandson was being named for her husband John and her father, Thomas, Cherokee Rose Chisholm cried.

"Hello, John Thomas Chisholm," she whispered. "Welcome to the world."

* * * * *

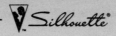

SPECIAL EDITION™

Coming in September 2004
from beloved author

ALLISON LEIGH

Home on the Ranch

(Silhouette Special Edition #1633)

When his daughter suffered a riding
accident, reclusive rancher Cage Buchanan
vowed to do anything to mend his daughter's
broken body and spirit. Even if that promise
meant hiring his enemy's daughter, Belle Day.
And though Cage thought Belle was the last
person he needed in his life, she drew him
like a moth to a flame....

Available at your favorite retail outlet.

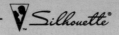

SPECIAL EDITION™

A Texas Tale

by

JUDITH LYONS

(Silhouette Special Edition #1637)

Crissy Albreit was a bona fide risk taker
as part of the daredevil troupe the
Alpine Angels. But Tate McCade was
offering a risk even Crissy wasn't sure
she wanted to take: move to Texas and
run the ranch her good-for-nothing
father left behind after his death. Crissy
long ago said goodbye to her past.
Now this McCade guy came bearing
a key to it? And maybe even one to
her future as well....

*Available September 2004
at your favorite retail outlet.*

If you enjoyed what you just read,
then we've got an offer you can't resist!

Take 2 bestselling love stories FREE!
Plus get a FREE surprise gift!

Martin

Silhouette®

COMING NEXT MONTH

#1633 HOME ON THE RANCH—Allison Leigh
Men of the Double S
Rancher Cage Buchanan would do anything to help his child—
even if it meant enlisting the aid of his enemy's daughter.
Beautiful Belle Day could no more ignore Cage's plea for help
than she could deny the passion that smoldered between them.
But could a long-buried secret undermine the happiness they'd
found in each other's arms?

#1634 THE RICH MAN'S SON—Judy Duarte
The Parks Empire
After prodigal heir Rowan Parks suffered a motorcycle accident,
single mom Luanne Brown took him in and tended to his wounds.
Bridled emotion soon led to unleashed love, but there was one
hitch: he couldn't remember his past—and she couldn't forget
hers....

#1635 THE BABY THEY BOTH LOVED—Nikki Benjamin
When writer Simon Gilmore discovered a son he never knew
was his, he had to fight the child's legal guardian, green-eyed
waitress Kit Davenport, for custody. Initially enemies, soon
Simon and Kit started to see each other in a new light. Would
the baby they both loved lead to one loving family?

#1636 A FATHER'S SACRIFICE—Karen Sandler
After years of battling his darkest demons, Jameson O'Connell
discovered that Nina Russo had mothered his chid. The world-
weary town outcast never forgot the passionate night that they
shared and was determined to be a father to his son...but could
his years of excruciating personal sacrifice finally earn him the
love of his life?

#1637 A TEXAS TALE—Judith Lyons
Rancher Tate McCade's mission was to get Crissy Albreit back
to the ranch her father wanted her to have. Not only did Tate's
brown-eyed assurance tempt Crissy back to the ranch she so
despised, but pretty soon he had her tempted into something
more...to be in his arms forever.

#1638 HER KIND OF COWBOY—Pat Warren
Jesse Calder had left Abby Martin with a promise to return...
but that had been five years ago. Now, the lies between them
may be more than Abby can forgive—even with the spark still
burning. Especially since this single mom is guarding a secret of
her own: a little girl with eyes an all-too-familiar shade of Calder
blue...

SSECNM0804